BLACK LIST

Next to barbed wire, there was nothing a cattleman hated more than sheep. It wasn't surprising then, that the ranchers in Hard Rock County would react in anger to Chance Abelard's decision to turn over a portion of his ranch to sheep herding.

Under the leadership of Pearce Jerome, owner of the largest ranch in the area, the Cowmen's Protective Association was formed. With the single exception of Chance Abelard, every rancher joined it. Tempers flared, and besides the threat of force, the Association meant to black-list Abelard's Two C Ranch.

It was a tough deal, but Chance Abelard knew he was right and meant to prove it—even if someone got hurt in the bloody fight that loomed ahead.

BLACK LIST

Giff Cheshire

GUNSMOKE

First published in the UK by Ward Lock

This hardback edition 2008
by BBC Audiobooks Ltd
by arrangement with
Golden West Literary Agency

ISBN 978 1 405 68225 1

British Library Cataloguing in Publication Data available.

Printed and bound in Great Britain by
CPI Antony Rowe, Chippenham, Wiltshire

Giff Cheshire was born in 1905 on a homestead in Cheshire, Oregon. The county was named for his grandfather who had crossed the plains in 1852 by wagon from Tennessee, and the homestead was the same one his grandfather had claimed upon his arrival. Cheshire's early life was colored by the atmosphere of the Old West which in the first decade of the century had not yet been modified by the automobile. He attended public schools in Junction City and, following high school, enlisted in the U.S. Marine Corps and saw duty in Central America. In 1929 he came to the Portland area in Oregon and from 1929 to 1943 worked for the U.S. Corps of Engineers. By 1944, after moving to Beaverton, Oregon, he found he could make a living writing Western and North-Western short fiction for the magazine market, and presently stories under the byline Giff Cheshire began appearing in *Lariat Story Magazine*, *Dime Western*, and *North-West Romances*. His short story *Strangers in the Evening* won the Zane Grey Award in 1949. Cheshire's Western fiction was characterized from the beginning by a wider historical panorama of the frontier than just cattle ranching and frequently the settings for his later novels are in his native Oregon. *Thunder on the Mountain* (1960) focuses on Chief Joseph and the Nez Perce War, while *Wenatchee Bend* (1966) and *A Mighty Big River* (1967) are among his best-known titles. However, his novels as Chad Merriman for Fawcett Gold Medal remain among his most popular works, notable for their complex characters, expert pacing, and authentic backgrounds. A first collection of Giff Cheshire's Western stories, *Renegade River*, was published in 1997 and edited by Bill Pronzini.

BLACK LIST

BLACK LIST

CHAPTER ONE

Ren Tyler glanced briefly at the street, seeing the weathered buildings of the town run irregularly down the one long thoroughfare and halt against the growing darkness of the flats. A mood of melancholy had grown out of the April rawness, but his deeper response was uneasiness because of the unusual number of saddle horses and wheeled rigs strung nearly the length of Alkali. He had had to hunt a place to rack his own horse and was walking back toward the telegraph office when he realized there was something going on at the lodge hall, whose doors were shut tight.

He saw her then, over in the doorway of Frankmeir's store and intently watching him—Libby Garnet. If she was in town, then her father was in the hall and probably as heated up over the new development as the rest of the Hard Rock country. When he caught Libby's eye, she turned her head with a toss that told him everything between them was over, unless he threw in his hand right now. She was a strong-tempered girl, and she had grown up on the back of a cow pony. He hesitated for only a moment before he walked along the street to the front of the mercantile, where she had climbed to the seat of a buckboard and was watching him troubledly.

He touched his hat, murmuring, "Howdy, Libby. Where's your dad?"

"At the hall."

"So he joined the association."

"He sure did."

She was nineteen now, and he had waited a long while for her to grow up, but it had been worth his time. The dark complexion that once had lent her the look of an Indian had turned into a sheer loveliness of brunette maturity, and the gangling body was now a slim and supple perfection. The difference in their ages no longer seemed so great, and for the moment he could only watch her, strangely moved and strongly regretful.

She broke the reserve, saying in sudden rebellion, "Why must you stick with it, Ren?" Her voice had the mellow timber of low flute notes.

"You know the answer to that, Libby," he said gently. "If his outfit's any good at all, a man sticks with it."

"Right or wrong?"

"Just like with his country."

"I don't see that!" she cried. "It's not the sheep. I can stand above prejudice, I think, the same as you must be doing because your heart can't be in it."

"Depends on how you look at it. I owe Chance plenty."

Furiously, she said, "Chance Abelard certainly knows he's starting a bloodletting. I've been fond of him, myself, but that's something I can't and won't excuse."

Ren shook his head. "Don't fault Chance if there's trouble, Libby. It's likely coming, but it'll be Pearce Jerome who starts it." He nodded downstreet. "He's organizing the Hard Rock right now, isn't he?"

"Yes, and the meeting'll be over in a minute. And if you're smart, you'll get out of town before it is."

"I've got business. Libby, those sheep won't be a threat to anybody in that hall. They'll run on our north edge, clean across our range from anybody else. Besides, they won't run loose, the way steers and horses do, so they might stray onto somebody. Chance's hired sheepherders, experts, and they'll be with 'em all the time. The rest of us're going to keep on working steers, the way we always have."

Her dark eyes snapped. "And if Chance gets away with this, what's to keep others from getting the sheep idea, people who won't be so considerate of the rest of us? Tramp sheepers like the Boscos, who'd like nothing better than slip in with their flocks and steal our grass. Oh, you fools—don't you see what you're doing?"

"Thought you claimed you can rise above prejudice," Ren retorted. "You're hollerin' about bloody trouble, but it sounds to me like you're trying to justify Pearce Jerome for starting it."

A voice behind him said, "Jerome don't need her help." Ren turned to see Joe Garnet standing there. He was tall, slender and dark as his daughter, but age had lined his face and sprinkled gray into his hair. The little outfit he ran was on Marsh Creek, up in the Dry Valley country and across the north basin from Abelard's Crank Creek setup. They had been good neighbors until now. "As to my own attitude," Garnet was continuing, "here it is. Turn sheeper, and my place is off bounds to you from here on. That clear?"

"Clear enough."

Ren looked to see if Libby agreed to her father's ultimatum, but she had turned her head.

He walked back up the street with a feeling of having been poleaxed. Out of the whole Hard Rock, they were the ones whose friendship it would hurt the worst to lose.

The lodge hall's doors were still emitting men, and as he met them he saw a raw hatred in some of their faces. Then, up ahead, he saw some Crown riders coming along with Pearce Jerome himself. Over on the far walk stood a hard-visaged handful from Cat Track, which adjoined Crown and would dance whenever Jerome cracked the whip. They were watching across the street to see what happened.

Jerome worked his way into the lead, his boot heels hammering the walk, and he stopped squarely in front of Ren, who saw in the late-day light a broad face unrelieved by tolerance or reasonableness, a mouth grown intensely bitter, and eyes angrily glowing. A strand of white hair fell from under a pushed-back hat, and shoulders unthinned by their age were pulled up to stress the hostile aggressions at work in the erect body. This was the Hard Rock's pioneer, its cattle king, regal, arrogant, and unchanging.

"Maybe you hear better than Chance Abelard seems to," Jerome said in angry energy. "He never listens to nobody, but you call yourself a cowhand and just might. You help him bring sheep into the Hard Rock, and you're through as such, and that goes for every jackdandy ridin' for you."

With unwonted calm, Ren said, "You got the wrong man, Pearce. I'm only the range boss at Two C. I don't make policy."

"And he can't carry out what he makes without you and your men. You know that. That damned cripple—"

"Easy, Pearce," Ren said gently, but his eyes had gone bleak.

Jerome's hand cut down. "You know he'd be helpless without you, and you're a damned fool to let him cost you like he will."

"What'll he cost me, Pearce?"

"If you care a damn about stayin' in the cattle business, that's what it'll cost. The minute Abelard brings sheep into the Hard Rock, he's goin' on the black list. You know what that means. No storekeeper in Alkali'll sell him a thing. Nobody'll buy his beef. And after he's gone busted, no other cow outfit in the West'll hire you and the men who help him in it. Think it over, Ren."

Jerome swung and walked on toward a tie rack taken over by Crown mounts, his crew behind him, their pride and confidence in their big ranch disclosed by their swinging arrogance. Cat Track moved up the other sidewalk in a body, and the hall was empty finally. Then old Pete Morse, the caretaker, appeared from inside to lock the doors, and Ren walked on to him.

"I take it they had a little meeting," Ren said, "in which my outfit come up for discussion."

"They did, and it did." The old man halted for a moment with his hand on the doorknob. "What you just seen walk out of here is the Cowmen's Protective Association. They all joined it—every big outfit in the Hard Rock save your Two C, and most of the little fellers. That's powerful odds, Ren. As a legal stockmen's association, they'll have the power to black-list you wherever cattle's run. Not only Chance Abelard but every forty-and-found puncher who stays on his payroll after this. They can make it stick, boy, and that's a lot to give up for the privilege of running a few woollies."

"It's the principle, Pete," Ren said hotly. "As to who tells Two C what it can do with its own range. The big grass is gone, and you set a saddle long enough yourself to see it. There's range in the Hard Rock so overgrazed by greedy men it won't support steers any more. But it will feed sheep, and they make money, and what Chance proposes, to pull his ranch back into the black, makes sense."

"Not to the ring-tailed snorters around here."

"They're hidebound, that's all."

A townsman came along the walk and pressed through the swinging doors of the saloon next to the hall. Ren knew him well, but the fellow gave no sign of it. Alkali would have to back the new association; it couldn't live off Two C's trade alone. A murmur of confused voices welled and faded as the doors vacillated to a stop. Ren caught the key word of the conversation.

Sheep.

Somberly, Pete Morse said, "Chance's asking a lot of you boys."

"No more'n he'd give us any time we needed it."

Ren walked on. They had hoped to get the sheep on their proposed range before the word spread, but Link Fowler and his mustangers had come back from a horse delivery to California with the news that Two C had bought a big flock down there to drive to the Hard Rock to run. The sheep still had to get here safely, and the association would do more about them than black-list the importing ranch. Just getting them through, the way the country was buzzing like hornets, could be a bloody business.

He turned into the telegraph office, where he found the wire he had come to town in hopes of getting. The telegrapher had sealed it in an envelope addressed to Chance, so Ren stuffed it in his pocket unopened and rode out through the sage and greasewood into the mounting night. He was a hard man, tall and rangy and bred to match this cattle domain under Oregon's high desert and along the border of California, but a strong foreboding went with him. His nerves were tight and ragged, not out of fear, but because he was throwing his past and future into the balance on what was bound to be the odiously unpopular side. And when it came to Libby Garnet—well, he had not declared his feelings to her yet, so she might not realize how deeply her contempt had hurt him.

When he had ridden steadily for some ten miles, the deepening night giving birth to a million stars, the valley pinched in, and over against the eastern hills, called the Pintos, he saw the dim, huddled lamplight of Narrows Ranch, now enemy territory. A few miles farther on the country opened into North Basin, and he rode on and reached home around midnight.

There was still a light in the main house, and when he had unsaddled and turned out his horse he crossed the ranch yard, thinking as he so often did that this place was as much a home to him as the one where he grew up. Cottonwoods shaded it, their roots watered by underground seeps of Crank Creek, which bisected the grounds, and the ranch, bunk- and cookhouses sat across from the noise and clutter of the barns, stables, and corrals. No woman had ever lived here, yet there was an air of tidiness incongruous to the twenty rough ranch hands who made this their headquarters.

He entered the house to find Chance Abelard waiting for him in the office. A man in his late fifties, the rancher sat at his desk, his shoulders as erect as when he had held a commission in the U. S. Army. But when he looked up Ren noted again the way his face sagged on one side and how the shoulder on the same side hung lower than the other, and he knew about the leg on that side, hidden by the desk, that had to be dragged as a useless appendage, all brought out of the Civil War. He knew about the intervening years, nearly thirty of them—put together from the little Chance ever said about them—in which he had reclaimed a devastated life just as he had built Two C out of near-wasteland.

Now the gaunt gray face made a change, the mobile side softening, smiling. "You're back promptly, Ren. Had the wire come in?"

Ren handed it over, watching the gray eyes that burned with so much intelligence and resolution while the older man ripped open the envelope and read the telegram. Then Chance looked up, his face granite again.

"I should have sent you in sooner. Lands is ahead of schedule. According to this, he'll have the sheep on the south end of Alkali Lake tomorrow."

Ren whistled. "Any trouble so far?"

"None he reported."

"There will be." Ren cuffed back his hat, took a chair, and reported what he had learned and been threatened with in Alkali. "You've handed Jerome what he's wanted for years," he concluded. "A good excuse to declare open war."

Chance rubbed his more active hand across his brow,

shaking his head, lost in long thoughts. After a moment, he said, "Well, it doesn't change much, really. He's made war of some sort on me for years. But I wish we could have got the sheep to Dry Gap before word got around. Now we'll have to move them through forty miles of hostile territory."

"We'll move 'em." Ren was aware of a strange, cold anger that had replaced his earlier tensions. How blind could people get, even in regard to their own welfare?

Chance knew, as Ren did, that the West was overstocked with cattle, which made the market ruinous to growers who depended on nothing but beef. So it had seemed sensible to look into sheep, which was something the Hard Rock would never forgive, apparently. And the more he learned the more he had seen in them the solution to the basin's financial difficulties. Sheep could thrive on range too poor to support cattle except for brief periods, and, handled always by herders, they could be controlled so as to complement, instead of competing with, a cattle operation. They produced two crops a year, wool and lamb, and the price of these was still high while beef had become a drug on the market. There wasn't an outfit in the country that couldn't profit if they would just give Chance the opportunity to demonstrate at his own risk what he had tried to tell them.

They had profited from Chance's pioneering before, if they would stop to remember. This country was part of an ancient volcanism that had given it a monolithic foundation, and faulting had shattered and tilted this basis, heaving up escarpments with long and gentle back-slopes covered with pine and bunch grass. The region was drained internally, the runoff pooling in lakes that evaporation had made unusable, but whose wheeling marshes grew wild hay in abundance. Before Chance's time no one had seen the enormous economic advantage in those stretching sour seeps and the sweet water from the uplands that each season was entirely lost in them.

Chance had been a laughingstock when, long before Ren's time, he had taken up a substantial range so poor nobody else had cared to bother with it, but in a few years this pilgrim with the fool notions had them laughing out of the other side of their mouths. It had been an enormous gamble in time, work, and money until it proved out, and he had gone on pure courage while he diverted his streams to new, natural storage basins and again while he ditched and drained the old seeps so they could sweeten into rich wild hay-lands. When the Hard Rock woke up to the fact that its hardscrabble outfit stood fair to become its showpiece, some of the other outfits had been willing to adopt his practices.

Not so Pearce Jerome.

Ren realized that Chance was looking at him troubledly. After a moment, the tired-looking man said, "You and the boys are going way out for me. Why?"

Embarrassed, because it was hard to voice the admiration that had compelled their loyalties, Ren said, "It's not such a gamble."

"Why not? Black-listing's a pretty deadly device. If we lose, you boys are finished with me."

"If we lose. But if we win we've got an even better ranch than the one we already liked to work for."

"Thanks. If it was only a matter of showing what can be done again, I wouldn't worry. In time we'd be forgiven, maybe even appreciated. But Jerome won't let me prove it. He'd rather die than see the old ways and ideas upset."

Ren's eyes narrowed. "When it comes to that, we'd drag our tails if you backed down for that old die-hard."

The live side of Chance's face softened in a smile. "Well, you'd better hit your blankets, because you'll have to meet Yancy Lands as early as possible tomorrow. He's flockmaster, and I'm told he's a damned good man and that the herders with him are no slouches. It seems a sheeper learns to be tough early or goes out of the business."

"Sometimes feet first. Good night, Chance."

"Good night, Ren. And one thing more. Make it clear to the boys that my chances are slim, the way it's shaping up. I don't expect them to gamble their futures, too, and if anybody wants his time in the morning he'll get it and no hard feelings."

"Sure, but don't look for many takers."

CHAPTER TWO

They rode in silence through the sage and greasewood under a blue April sky, heading southward toward low finger mountains lying bright in the unfiltered sun. They wore puncher's clothes, and six-shooters hung at each saddle-leaned hip to round out the grimness of their dust-grayed faces. The trail they had followed since morning ran between the Kettle Hills and the Indian reserve, a backway from Two C to the border country. In spite of the solitude, the riders watched the changing scenery with the hard scrutiny born of warning.

The puncher riding beside Ren Tyler was a thin, shaggy-haired man and his *segundo*—Gila Veyan, who over the years had disclosed much more of himself in action than in word of mouth. When he broke the heavy silence, Gila's voice showed the abrasion of chemicals kicked up by the horses as they circled the long, impregnated margin of Alkali Lake.

"Yonder's a dust. That the sheep?"

The forecountry was rock-strewn and brushy, and deep in the purpled south a sooty puff faintly daubed the horizon.

The white rings around Ren's eyes lent his features a look of ferocity, and he sat his saddle as tightly as if a magnet pulled him to it. "Not big enough a dust," he said.

"Likewise, it could be going instead of coming."

"And if it's going, it could spell trouble. Let's take a look."

He had left Two C at daybreak with five picked men, and the other four were divided into pairs like himself and Gila, each making its separate way to a rendezvous on south of Massacre Pass to avoid the effect a large group of armed black-list riders might have on the aroused countryside. Now he and Gila went loping forward, a hard impassivity again setting their faces, and he was thinking with satisfaction that not a man had accepted Chance's offer and drawn his pay.

Gila called presently, "Dust's keeping ahead. You reckon the association's sent a reception committee?"

"There's a three to one chance."

A mile later they reined in for another hard look at the obscure distance. The dust had kept receding about as fast as they traveled themselves, eliminating a wheeled rig, so they put their horses to a gallop to close the gap. A few minutes later they cut a fresh trail that led in from the northeast. There were too many horse tracks, too compactly stamped, for that to be a riding party up there.

"Bronc herd," Ren called. "That's Link Fowler and his stompers."

Gila's eyes narrowed. Of all the men in the Hard Rock with reason to hate Fowler, none had a greater one than his. The thin man turned his head and spat dust from his mouth. He called in a toneless voice, "Moving two herds into California in a row? That's pretty frequent."

"Too damned frequent. He aims to run those wild horses through the flock and make some mutton sausage."

They whipped and spurred their horses, now, as they drove on at breakneck speed, and when they topped the next land swell they saw ahead of them a band of about a hundred mustangs being hazed along the trail and pressing steadily into the south. Two riders followed them, and, while the dust cut them from sight, Ren knew there would be more on the flanks and point, too many for him and Gila to dispute effectively, whatever their intentions. The rendezvous with his four other riders was several miles farther south. The best thing was to get ahead of Fowler, unite his own outfit, and then do what had to be done.

One of the forward riders swung his horse and pulled it to a stop. The shape of the man and coloration of the horse told Ren it was Fowler on his favorite mount, a stallion he had trapped in the breaks of Wild Horse Plateau. A scowl stained the mustanger's hawk-sharp face when the Two C riders whipped up to him and reined in. A couple of his stompers were holding back, on ahead, to be near if they were needed. All three were heavily armed, and Ren knew they were ready to mix it.

"What's the idea barrelin' in on a herd of broncs?" Fowler demanded. "Don't you know any better?"

"Know enough to wonder where you're heading, Link," Ren retorted. "Supposing you satisfy our curiosity."

"Not that it's any of your business, but we're going to the Sacramento."

"You just come back from there."

"This is a double delivery."

Fowler's manner was surly, but Ren detected an overtone of malicious amusement. He was dust-coated, raggedly dressed, and his shoulders were surprisingly wide and powerful for a man so tall and slender. He had a horse setup north of Jerome's Crown and, while he ran a few steers, his work was mainly the breaking and selling of the wild horses he and his hard cases trapped in the breaks. Watching Ren steadily, the mustanger let his lips peel back in a grin that belied his claim. He wanted his insolence and intentions to be realized.

"Cut it, Link," Ren said angrily. "The order you're filling this trip come straight from Pearce Jerome. You're not stampeding your *oreanas* through those sheep. Not this time."

"Stampede my cayuses? Not me, Ren. It was too much work catchin' and breakin' 'em. What got you boys so exercised? We're only trailing to market, like we do right along."

"Timed so you'll meet the sheep about Massacre Pass. Huh-uh, Link. It would give you a nice excuse for a bloody mix-up, but you're not going to do it."

"What am I going to do?"

"Hold up till the woollies get through the pass or wait so I can turn 'em off trail and let you through first."

With a look of elaborate regret, Fowler shook his head. "I just can't hold up, Ren, much as I'd like to oblige you. I'm late with this delivery, already, and the customer's kickin' about it."

Ren caught Gila's eye and knew that the old bitterness between him and Fowler was about ready to start action on its own. He nodded and, saying no more to Fowler, rode on, and Gila followed.

Thereafter they cut wide of the steadily traveling mustangs and pulled ahead of the band. They crossed a ridge, then the state line was only a little way ahead. Beyond it a stringer mountain lay naked on the horizon, bisected by a deep and sharply beveled canyon. That was Massacre Pass where, long ago, the Indians had wiped out a train of emigrants bound for the California gold fields. The riders reined in.

"Somebody worked out a real cute caper," Gila said moodily. "Nobody could fault Fowler if a band of sheep showed up ahead of him in the pass where it couldn't help get steam-rollered by his wild horses. And that's what's gonna happen, if we don't stop it. They must have had spies watching the woollies."

"Afraid so," Ren agreed.

"What'd we better do?"

"Keep Fowler out of the pass till we're sure the sheep aren't in it."

"We'd have to stampede his critters."

"Which is what we're gonna do."

It had been a hard decision, yet they had been given no choice but to make the first hostile move in what already seemed sure to build into a bitter blood feud. Caught by the horses in the miles-long constriction of the pass, the sheep could not escape slaughter, and Ren agreed with Gila that Fowler had timed himself to accomplish that. He swung his mount to see that the wild horses had topped the rearward ridge and were within a half mile of them.

"Listen!" Gila hissed.

The ragged blatting of distant sheep came to them, thrown forward by the high rock walls of the pass.

The mustangers could not have heard the sheep, but the threat of the men at the mouth of the pass was soon clear enough. Fowler's point riders boiled forward to ward off any danger to the horse herd and clear the pass so the band could be fanned in. Ren jerked up his six-shooter and set a bullet whistling toward them to warn that they could not approach the canyon without a contest, hoping the possibility of a horse stampede would turn Fowler aside voluntarily.

The only effect was a ripple of uneasiness that stirred through the oncoming band, which was controlled not only by the men but by an admixture of well-broken horses. The riders still with it tightened up, and answering shots crackled through the bright heat of the afternoon. A horseman bulged out of the dusty flanks, jerking a rifle to his shoulder, and Ren recognized Fowler. The warning was being defied.

"They're askin' for it, Gila," Ren said gustily, and spurred his horse.

It was a reckless charge, for the rapidly shooting mustangers aimed in dead earnest while the Two C riders thundered head-on toward the herd of skittish horse flesh, firing over the animals, and shouting themselves hoarse. It was a display of courage Fowler had not credited them with possessing, and it was already too late for him to tighten his scattered men enough to hold the band together. For a moment the

Two C punchers seemed about to hurl themselves straight into the oncoming mass, then panic hit the wildlings, and they wheeled as one and went driving to the east.

Fowler's shouts came punching through the racket, "Hold 'em! Boys, get around 'em!"

He had waited too long. The gentled horses mixed with the wild ones were swept along in the rush, and the herders had let themselves scatter so that the streaking animals slipped out of control and were free. They represented too much work and market value for Fowler to be willing to let them go and concentrate his attention on the men who had ruined his plans. He took his crew thundering off, trying desperately to regain control of the escaped band.

"That gives us a breather," Gila panted.

"We'll need more than that," Ren told him. "The woollies're still days from Dry Gap."

They could hear their helpless charges again, complaining as they came on through the canyon passage.

As Ren turned back with Gila toward the portal, a man rode out of it, a rifle held at ready, his uneasy alertness telegraphed by a darting survey of the foreground. Ren swung his hat in a circle above his head, then rode on to meet the man.

"Howdy," he said, when they joined up. "I take it you're Yancy Lands. We're Abelard hands from Two C, here to escort you in. I'm Ren Tyler, and this is Gila Veyan."

The flockmaster was far from what he had expected, a man of his own strapping build and no older than himself who bore none of the earmarks commonly associated with a sheepherder. He rode a fine horse as if he belonged on its back and wore a six-shooter in addition to the Winchester he carried. A smile broke the sternness of his face while he shook hands. "I took it from the shooting that I had friends out here," he commented. "Who gave you trouble?"

"Another bunch with intentions a little different than ours.

Some men with wild horses they aimed to have meet you in the canyon."

"Phew. I'm obliged for the help."

At that moment a belled billy came out of the canyon, and behind it the first blatting sheep. They were newly sheared, and Ren knew there would be three flocks of ewes and lambs and a separate buck band, nearly nine thousand head in all. The dusty gray mass began to widen outside the canyon, like water fanning over a flat, and then the end of the first flock was marked when a walking herder emerged with his dog.

"How far to this Dry Gap?" Lands asked.

"Forty miles on the back trail we'll take. How fast can you push 'em?"

"Ten-twelve miles a day, feeding as we go. Sheep trail pretty much like steers."

"You've worked cattle?"

Lands laughed. "Up to five years ago you couldn't have hired me to even look at a sheep."

"What changed your attitude?"

"I went broke on cattle."

Ren wished Pearce Jerome had heard that, and his respect for this laconic ex-cattleman was already considerable. Gila's eyes showed that he was likewise impressed.

For what seemed an interminable time, sheep gushed from the canyon, bleating a constant protest and fouling the air with a heavy dust, an occasional break occurring in which another half-choked herder and dog appeared. Lands fanned the herders and their animal helpers on and remained there with the Two C punchers until finally three sheep wagons and a cavvy of extra horses came into view.

"I scouted this section yesterday," he said. "We'll camp a few miles on north."

"I've got four more men coming," Ren told him. "They

kept to the side, so me and Gila got ahead of 'em. We'll join up and check on those mustangers."

"Got grub and such?" Lands asked. "We've plenty, and you're welcome."

"One of my boys is bringing a pack pony. We figured to be out a few days."

The flockmaster rode on after his sheep. Swinging east with Gila for two miles, Ren came to Wagonhub Springs, where Jim Fanning and Flint Hollister waited with the camp pack. They had a belated noon meal, and, before they had finished, Abe Jewett and Frank Watson rode in. They were all young men but old Two C hands, and if anybody could keep Fowler's tough hirelings away from the sheep, they could.

Ren outlined his plan for the rest of the escort. "Fowler's got two-three thousand dollars' worth of horse flesh in that band, and we'll keep him so all-fired busy defending it he can't think of anything else. But he'll send word to Pearce Jerome, if he can't get at the sheep himself, which'll give us something new and different to think about."

"With the enemies this business is makin' for us," Jim Fanning said moodily, "they could wipe us out with one swipe if they wanted."

Ren shook his head. "I don't figure they'll want it that messy. The whole reason for organizing that cowmen's association was to gain help from other organizations and the business people. Something like an accidental collision between the woollies and Fowler's mustangs would be all right, but if they got too outright raw they'd risk losing support. Well, let's pack up and find the *oreanas*."

They left Fanning to bring on the pack, and the other five rode south and cut the trail of the fleeing wild-horse band. The mustangs had followed the rimmed base of the mountain, holding together as even stampeding wild horses did, but it was evident that the Fowler outfit had been given a long, hard ride. The brushy, rock-crusted terrain was difficult at even a moderate speed, and the Two C party did not crowd it recklessly. After a few miles, the country began to roll in low rises and yawning hollows, and then, some ten miles east of Massacre Pass, they came over a crown and saw the band below them in a saucer.

"They nailed 'em, finally," Gila said, "but it took as much ginger out of the mustangers as from the mustangs. Better go easy, Ren. They'll see us in a minute."

"Want 'em to," Ren said. "We're gonna wolf-watch 'em."

They rode on until in plain view, then he called a halt. By then the men below were aware of their presence and watching them uneasily. They had outrun their camp and must be famished, as well as worn down and worried. It had been shown them that they also were vulnerable, and Fowler wanted no repetition of what had happened at the pass. Ren and his men dismounted, trailed reins, and rolled smokes, hunkering at their ease in the shade of their mounts.

Ren watched the belowground with satisfaction in the turn of the table, although he knew that his advantage was fleeting. There was a notable dejection in the men slowly circling the tired mustangs, letting them rest and quiet down before attempting to move them again. He kept track of Link Fowler easily by the markings of his stallion, and presently Fowler stopped to let another rider catch up with him. They talked for a moment, then Fowler seemed to call an order, for the other riders alerted and began to edge in on the band.

"Decided to get crackin'," Gila said at Ren's elbow. "Heading west again. For the pass or for the sheep?"

"We'll try to influence their judgment."

As soon as the wildlings were lined out, picking back over the course of the long run, Two C rose to saddle and started in the same direction, keeping on the sky line and ready at any moment to ball things up again. Fanning caught up, bringing the camp pack, which advised the mustangers that this wolf-watch could continue a long while. The effect was cogent, for Fowler kept a steady eye on them throughout the two hours, afterward, in which the horse band moved tiredly westward. Then they were back on the California trail, and the mustangs turned south.

"He's goin' into the pass with 'em!" Watson said gleefully. "He's had all he wants of our medicine!"

"We only won a skirmish, boys," Ren warned, although he felt considerably relieved himself.

They remained immobile as skulking lobos waiting to close in on a weakened prey until the mustangers had fanned the last of the band into the pass and disappeared. The sun by then had dropped well toward the horizon, and Two C had had a long, tense day in the saddle, itself.

Turning to Gila, Ren said, "You might as well take the boys back to the sheep camp for the night. Me, I'm gonna stay here and watch that canyon mouth awhile."

"How come?"

"Fowler'll try to get word to Jerome to take over for him. He couldn't send anybody back with us watchin' because we'd stop him. He'll try it, though, after dark. Go in and get some chuck, and if I'm not in by midnight, bring me something to eat. He might wait till well into the night before he tries it."

"Let me wait and hope Link tries it himself. I'd sure like a chance like that. Just me and Link Fowler."

"That wouldn't help her any, Gila," Ren said gently. "Get on, now. Get a bait of grub and some rest."

CHAPTER THREE

Ren rode north with his men until a ridge had cut him from view of the pass, where Fowler or one of his men would be watching to see what Two C did next. The light weakened swiftly, and over the rise Ren turned off the trail and headed west toward a juniper-covered knob. Reaching the thin timber, he climbed until he could again see the mouth of the pass. Once there he dismounted, loosened the saddle cinch, and took the bit from his horse's mouth. Afterward he found a better viewpoint and sat down there to smoke a cigarette, watching the night close in. No other wayfarers came out of the pass or moved toward it from the Hard Rock, and the wild silence began to lull and loosen him.

He wondered if Link Fowler realized the hatred Gila bore him. Everyone knew his daughter's story and what Link had done to her in punishment for her one defiant act. Most of the Hard Rock felt sorry for Rita Fowler and would help her if they could, but with Gila it was a riding obsession. Gila would long since have killed him if Fowler had not found a cruel and clever way to protect himself from her friends.

When it grew too dark to see the pass from the distance, Ren remounted and rode down to the trail, along which a rider would have to come to reach Jerome's spread in the east basin. Immediately he struck south and toward the pass, concealed in the deepened darkness before the stars came out, and he reached the pass and entered it. There would be no chance for a Fowler man to elude or outrun him in there, and he rode to the first dog-leg turn and, on its blind side, stopped and dismounted to wait again.

He no longer dared risk lighting a smoke, and fatigue grew so heavy he had trouble keeping alert. Stars emerged in a fiery stripe above the rocky walls, and at last it came: the swift strike of hoofs along the canyon floor to the south. He swung into saddle and rode out to stop squarely on the trail, his gun gripped in his fingers and his attention fixed on the jutting face of rock around which the rider must come. The walls made the hoofbeat like the punch of fast shooting, swelling toward him, then horse and its silhouetted burden whipped around the jut, just ahead. He fired a high-angled shot.

"Hold it!" he shouted. "And don't try anything!"

The onrushing horse skidded to a stop, throwing forward a dust burst that would have helped the rider's gunplay had surprise not braked his reactions. Even so, the man jabbed a hand at the grips of his weapon, but recovered and lifted his arms hastily.

"Ren Tyler!" he gasped.

Ren had recognized him by then and said, "Thought you were deliverin' mustangs to the Sacramento, Hunk. That's in the other direction."

Hunk Roddy's main ambition was to reflect, as faithfully as his limitations permitted, the qualities he admired in Link Fowler. He was as powerful physically and as callous emotionally, and what he lacked in brain power Fowler was able to supply.

"You tricky bastard!" Roddy grated.

"Loosen the shell belt, Hunk, and hand over the rig. Easy with it. I'd rather kill than have you on my hands to worry about."

"What're you doin' with me?"

"Making sure you don't pay a visit to Crown tonight, or for the next several days. Get moving, damn you. I haven't had my supper because of you, and I'm plenty cross about it."

Roddy surrendered his weapon in surly submission, then at Ren's command passed ahead and rode out of the canyon. Starshine brightened the open reaches, so Ren ordered his prisoner to go on at a trot. They left the trail where it bent to circle the big lake bed and took the western route, which the flocks had followed. In about half an hour they reached the sheep camp.

The only sheepmen there with the Two C riders were Yancy Lands and an old Mexican *cocinero*. The punchers were bedded down, and it was still short of the midnight Gila was supposed to wait for before riding to the pass with food. Gila and Lands had been sitting by the fire, but were on their feet when Ren rode in with Roddy.

"So you got your coyote," Gila said with a wicked laugh.

"Hobble him," Ren said briefly. "He's gonna be your guest a few days, Lands."

"Then he better like mutton," the flockmaster said, and grinned at Roddy's curse.

Ren unsaddled and put his horse on picket, and when he walked back to the fire, Lands offered him a plate of beans, with biscuits and coffee but no mutton. His herders slept with their flocks, he explained, and their highly trained dogs would keep them from being surprised by enemies.

His hunger appeased, Ren lighted a smoke and leaned back against a rock. "With Roddy in our hands," he told Lands, "Fowler and Jerome will leave it to each other to take care of us. If we can keep it so about three more days, we're out of the worst danger. The strip you're following's a no man's land that's never used except for driving stock. It's dry, and the hills cut it off from the main grazing ranges, and it's too close to the Indian reserve for it to be safe to leave steers on unwatched. But the Indians won't bother us just goin' through, so if trouble comes it'll be through the hills from the main Hard Rock. Me and my men'll watch out for that."

Nodding, Lands said, "How long does this last?"

"Three days should put you to a break in the hills they call Warbonnet Gap. That's our next danger point, if Jerome gets wind of what's happened in spite of us holding Roddy. But if we make it through the gap, we'll be on Two C range. Not apt to be molested for the one more day you'll need to reach Dry Gap ranch."

"What's at Dry Gap?"

"Used to be headquarters of a little cow outfit till Abelard bought it a while back for this sheep experiment. There's a shack, a barn and some corrals, with plenty of water in winter and damned little in summer. Some of the boys're putting in time, till calf roundup, getting out poles and posts for your sheeppens and sheds. There's a hay marsh there the old outfit let the steers feed on in winter. We'll cut, cure and stack the hay, plenty to winter your flocks."

"Where's the grazing range?" Lands asked.

"At first you'll go up to the high desert with the critters. Grass up there'll be good till the hot winds hit in July. Then you'll come down on the marsh stubble after haying, and move from there to the feed lots at Dry Gap when real winter hits. In early spring you start the round over, goin' back to the high desert."

"Sounds like a good setup."

"The boss thinks so, and usually he's dead right. But you know by now that the other outfits in the Hard Rock think it's gonna be a real stinkpot."

Wryly, Lands said, "I sort of gathered that at the pass."

Ren went on, explaining the cattle setups in the adjoining country which would not be bothered in any way except in their own minds. He described the people involved and other things he thought Lands ought to know. Meanwhile, his liking for the man increased. By common standards, Lands was degenerate, a man who had quit the cattle business to turn sheep nurse. But Ren would have defied anybody to call Yancy Lands a weakling, particularly in the man's hearing.

He wakened at daylight to find the *cocinero* had breakfast ready, and that the herders were appearing in relays to eat. He met a couple of them, Ben Corbett and Si Botwood, oldtimers in the sheep business who looked upon him and his cowhands with lingering suspicion. Lands had disappeared from the camp, and the herders said the flocks were already moving on north. Ren hurried his own men through their meal, assured that the sheepmen needed nothing from him beyond help in fending off molestation while they had their hands full with the drive. He was convinced that they would be less than helpless even in that respect.

Leaving a man to guard Roddy, Ren took the others and rode into the hills, taking his camp pack. This range, which formed the west border of the Hard Rock, was called the Kettles and provided summer grass for the outfits in the north and south basins. If trouble came despite the steps he had taken, he wanted to detect and meet it as far from the sheep as he could. After two hours they reached the ridge line, along which ran an ancient Indian trail. He began to drop off men at intervals that each of them was to patrol, watching for sign of men crossing the ridge in numbers. He took the pack on to a point opposite where Lands would camp that night. There he unloaded, tethered, and left the pack pony.

He rode swiftly through the hills, thereafter, aimed northeast, and in midmorning came to Rooster Head Peak. This was the highest point of land in the Hard Rock, rearing a thousand feet above the north basin's flat floor. There he dismounted to sit on his heels and smoke a cigarette, enjoying the scene below him for its space and magnificent austerity.

Far to the east rose the sheer, sky-reaching rampart of Pinto Scarp, the dividing formation between this valley and the east basin, which Jerome's Crown outfit dominated. To the south the near basin pinched in to form the narrows, and from there, reaching northward under the escarpment, was Dry Lake, a vast arid bed of mineral-impregnated soil except at its southern tip. The northern end of the waste disappeared behind Bloody Rim, a detached mesa thrust up from the flat floor. The climbing sun brought out the pigmentation that made these bluffs a dripping red.

The heart of Two C range lay directly below him, a broad, ten-mile stretch of marshland that received the flow of Crank Creek, once waste that had been fertile soil the past twenty years. In another three months a traveling hay outfit would come in, and he could all but see the staggered line of mowers creeping across the enormous marsh. Rakers would work behind them, and in the rear would come the big slips that sledded the hay to the baler, storing nourishment sufficient to hold Two C's herd and horses through the hardest of winter months.

Presently he rose to saddle and swung back to the head of Crank Creek and dropped into its valley, a flat-bottomed finger that probed deep into the Kettles and sheltered the livestock even in the severest blizzards. He rode on for another two hours and at noon came to Two C headquarters, where the creek began a horseshoe bend toward the marshlands.

Chance was in his office, waiting, his window having let him see the arrival. "You're all one piece," he commented, the robust side of his face grinning. "How'd it go?"

Ren shoved back his hat and took a chair. "Good and bad, which is what I come in about. The sheep are safe on the strip, but we tangled with Link Fowler at Massacre Pass.

He was making for there with a bronc herd he claimed he was delivering to California. It was my notion—as his actions proved—that he aimed to catch the sheep in the canyon and barrel those mustangs over 'em."

Chance's expressive eye narrowed. "So?"

"So we stampeded the mustangs and made Two C the first to get rough in this hassle. That'll count against us."

"I expect, but if I'd been there, that's what I'd have told you to do. So Jerome used Fowler."

"That worries me, too. Not what Fowler'll do about the trouble we gave him, but Jerome's throwing him against us the first rattle out of the box. I don't like the look of that."

"Jerome had his reasons."

Ren nodded. "Yeah. Fowler thrives on dirty work and usually don't get enough to satisfy him. On the other hand, Crown and the new association's got to look as good as possible. This business has started a personal feud between Fowler and us, and Jerome'll let him carry the fight to us, at least the dirty part."

"Which'll be dirty as hell if Fowler stays in character. Which he will. He hasn't changed in the last twenty years that I know of."

Ren went on to describe how he had intercepted the man dispatched by the mustanger to tell Jerome that the sally had failed so Crown could take over. They talked a while longer about other problems facing them, and Ren reported that Lands and his herders could hold up their end any time. He knew he had eased Chance's mind considerably, which made the long ride down here worth-while.

Afterward he went to the cookhouse for the noon meal, finding only a few of the hands there to share it, for the bulk of the crew was staying at Dry Gap ranch and cutting poles on Bloody Rim for the new sheep structures. He ate thoughtfully, reflecting that Chance had once had a few real friends in the Hard Rock, little operators who had been willing to learn and profit from the improved methods he had worked out. One such was Joe Garnet, Libby's father, but Joe had made his present sentiments plenty clear.

Another was Varley Eden, whose headquarters were at the narrows, a man whose fortunes had improved after Chance persuaded him to convert the sink of Two Hour Creek into a producer of hay. Varley would remember that and might be holding a more open mind about the newest Two C experiment. It occurred to Ren that he could swing down to the narrows on his way back to the ridge patrol and still make it before night fell.

Two hours later he turned off the Alkali road toward Eden's little huddle of buildings. Eden was there when he rode in, framed in the doorway of the shack that stood at the edge of a cluttered ranch yard. His eyes were sullen, startling Ren with the realization of how powerful an emotion ingrained intolerance could be and how closed were the minds that harbored it. He knew already that he might as well have saved himself the extra ride.

When Eden offered no greeting, Ren kept saddle, his horse drawn up below the porch. Reaching for tobacco and papers, he said, "I see you've got your dander up as high as the rest, Varley. Didn't happen to see you in town the other day, but I guess you joined the association."

"I joined it."

"Expectin' to help yourself?"

"Figurin' to keep sheep from ruinin' this country."

"You might stop to wonder just what it is that's threatening it." Ren troughed a paper and tapped tobacco into it. "Know who Jerome's made the strong right arm of your association? Link Fowler. How come you'd trust him more than Chance Abelard, I don't know. You little fellows don't seem to realize what your program could cost you. You won't run it. Jerome will, and the rest of you'll never be sure what he and Fowler are up to. You'll dance to the tune they call, and they just might leave you to pay the fiddler. Think it over." Ren turned his horse.

A stooped man who had once been huge, Eden lifted a hand. "Just a minute. What's Fowler done that's so bad?"

"Tried to stampede a band of mustangs through the sheep."

"And that's bad?"

Eden laughed.

Ren gave him a long, thoughtful glance, then rode on. He had credited Eden and Garnet with horse sense, but they seemed to fear the upset of their fixed ideas as much as the other basiners did. What a threat to them that was when cunning men could callously use it to their own selfish ends.

CHAPTER FOUR

Warbonnet Gap, when the sheep reached it on the third day, seemed so placid to Gila Veyan, and so devoid of trouble, that the wearing days of tension appeared to have been unwarranted. But he knew they had not been. The peaceful passage through the pass and on to Dry Gap only proved that Two C had succeeded in throwing both Fowler and Jerome off stride and nothing more. When the truth dawned, as it must, they would buzz around like hornets, infuriated by the defeat and all the more determined to bring the Crank Creek outfit to its knees.

Hunk Roddy had the look of a surly captive bear when Ren finally ordered him turned loose. "Go on and deliver your message to Jerome," the range boss told him. "If they don't run you off Crown for your sorry performance, they'll laugh you off, and I wish I could see it."

Roddy turned to the horse that had been restored to him and swung into the saddle. For a moment his eyes burned into those watching him. "Nobody gives me a deal like this," he said bitterly, "and gets away with it. I'll make you jiggers pay for every damn' day you held onto me. So help me, I will."

"Yonder's the horizon," Gila said calmly. "Knock a hole in it, Hunk."

When they were alone, Yancy Lands shook his head. "If

his hired hand is any sample, Link Fowler's a mighty fragrant hombre."

"Link could give Roddy the first squirt," Ren said, "and still outskunk him."

Gila waited restlessly, goaded by something he wanted to do and held to patience because he would have to do it secretly. He had not overcome his own ingrained dislike of sheep, and it puzzled him why Lands had swung over to them so completely as to become a flockmaster, but he had developed considerable respect for the man. He sat his saddle, listening idly to the talk between Lands and Ren, mildly interested in what the sheep operation would be from there on. The next day, Ren was saying, he would show the flock- master the high desert range. Afterward, Lands intended to cut the flock into three or four bands, sending them into separate areas, each with a sheep wagon, two herders, and a pair of the highly trained dogs. The wagons would be supplied by a camp tender based at Dry Gap, and Lands would spend his own time supervising the grazing and the pen building at the gap, which would have to be finished before winter.

Gila stirred, when finally Ren turned to him and said, "Reckon I'll spend the night here so me and Lands can get off to an early start in the morning. You and the boys might as well ride in to headquarters. Next on dock for us is calf roundup."

Nodding, Gila said, "Since we're over this far, how about me riding on to the Split Rock camp to see how the boys there're doing?" That was a section on the east edge of Two C's range where some steers had been turned loose in late winter, with a couple of punchers staying there temporarily to take care of them.

"Sure," Ren said, although Gila had been afraid he would see through it. "The boys ought to be posted on what's happening. They're settin' pretty close to Fowler's horse out- fit. You'd better stay overnight."

"That's what I figured," Gila agreed.

Ten minutes later he was riding through the late afternoon. He was already east of Bloody Rim in what was known as Dry Valley, and far to the south he could see the near end of Dry Lake. The Split Rock camp was between the lake and Turkey Neck Ridge, a narrow upland that connected the Pinto and Turkey Head hills. But he had something to do before he finally hit the camp for the night, something that now wholly filled his mind.

Instead of swinging south when he came in under the ridge, he struck directly onto it, following a trail that led into East Basin. In about an hour he topped the ridge, coming to a high point from which he could see awesome sweeps of the basins before and behind him, now lying in the softening light of the evening. Yet, when he reined in to blow his horse, he sat facing eastward, seeing below him the line of cotton-woods that marked the length of Deacon Creek and, well out in the basin, the marshland and necklace-string of alkali lakes that ran nearly twenty miles to the south. There, where Deacon Creek entered the marsh, was Link Fowler's head-quarters, and down the basin about ten miles lay Crown.

It was probable that Hunk Roddy had headed directly for Crown instead of going to the horse ranch, because Crown was the only place he could get help until Fowler and the other mustangers got back from California. That would leave no one at the horse ranch but Rita and the half-wit her father relied upon to keep her isolated during his frequent absences. Gila knew the whole horse setup inti-mately. He had worked for Fowler his first year in the Hard Rock, he and his *muy amigo*, Wad Wadsworth.

He could see no rider anywhere in view below him and presently began a back-switching descent into the east basin, emerging at last among the creek's thick cottonwoods. The day's last light was retreating swiftly before the onset of dusk, and he rode with some confidence along the course of the creek, not leaving the trees until he was within a mile of the horse ranch headquarters. By then it was sufficiently dark for him to make a direct ride to the back side of the cuesta against which the buildings were set on its bluff side. He left his horse, then, and climbed on afoot to the rim, mounting the easy backslope.

Rita needed no guard for she would never try to run away voluntarily, and the simple-minded giant, known only as Meathead and completely subdued by Fowler and obedient to him only, served mainly to keep other men away from her. Meathead was alert as an Indian, and for all his thick wits was remarkably keen in vision and hearing. Gila lay on the rim, studying the buildings below him, determined to see Rita before her father got back from his trip.

There was lamplight in the house, an ugly, unpainted structure no woman but Rita had ever been forced to live in since her mother died when she was a baby. The bunkhouse was also palely lighted, as if by a single smoky lantern, and Meathead would be there, for all the sheds and corrals were dark and deserted. Gila would have taken pleasure in dealing with the hulking giant directly, but that was out of the question. He dared do nothing that would rouse Fowler's smoldering suspicion and resentment of his daughter.

He lay waiting on the rim top, hoping Meathead would go to bed early and thus be a little less attentive to the night's sounds and movements, and he thought of those other nights, five years before, when Rita had been slipping out to meet Wad Wadsworth. There had been no Meathead then, just her father's determination to keep men away from her and her away from men, but the moment she and Wad saw each other they had fallen in love. What followed, on their part, had been natural, inevitable. Only Fowler's reactions had been depraved and terrible.

A night breeze was coming up in the basin, blown from the vastness of Wild Horse Plateau and its yawning breaks.

The stars began to pop out in countless light bursts, and presently Meathead's shadow showed on a bunkhouse window. A moment later thin light spilled from an opened door, and the giant appeared in the yard and stood motionless, taking a long look around. Then he went back inside, the door closed, and the light went out.

Gila waited another ten minutes, then rose and retreated quietly down the slope and came around the west end of the cuesta. Very carefully, afterward, he made his way through the tangled system of corrals and horse-breaking traps and came in on the main house on the side opposite Meathead's quarters. Long ago he had learned Wad's signal, which Rita had recognized on the other occasions he had dared this visit himself. He came up under a darkened window he knew to be her bedroom, and there began another wait.

This one was not long, for presently a light appeared vaguely beyond the windowpane. When he knew she had come into her room, he rapped on the glass, twice slowly and twice fast. He had repeated this when the light went abruptly out and, in a moment, the window sash lifted up.

"That you, Gila?" her whispered voice said.

"Yes, Rita."

"You oughtn't—"

"Meathead's in his soogans, and the others are a long way from here. I had to see you, Rita. You all right?"

"I get along."

He had never tried to go through that window, although he knew how desperately lonely she was, how hungry for friendship, for talk, and understanding. He remained in the darkness beside the house and could see her vaguely, although he knew her appearance so well she seemed brightly illuminated. A dark girl, a slender, supple, lovely girl whose only associates were the roughest, lowest men in the Hard Rock. He felt the band on his throat that always tightened when he thought of her and her life.

"I wanted to tell you," he whispered, "that trouble's starting. So help me, I'll find a way in it to make him tell me where the boy is. When he does, you'll be free. I'll help you get away. Anything. You know that, don't you?"

He wondered if the child looked like Wad, curly-haired and merry-eyed. He hoped so, that there was something of Wad left in the world for Rita, even though they didn't know where.

She was a long moment in whispering, "I know you want to, Gila, but you can't help me. Nothing can. He won't give me back my baby. I used to think he would if I did what he wanted. But he won't. I sinned, he says, and I've got to pay for it."

"If you sinned, hell wouldn't have Link Fowler and his cronies. You trust me, Rita, and be patient. I'll find a way."

"You'll only get yourself killed like Wad did."

"Don't worry about that. *Adios*, now. I'll see you again the first chance I get."

"Be careful—and, Gila?"

"Yeah?"

"I'm obliged."

He turned and slipped off into the shadows, pausing at the corner of the barn to make certain Meathead had not been aroused, then he faded on along the alleys between the corrals and made his way back to his horse. It outraged him that Rita had come to accept hopelessness as her lot, even though he had tried so hard to keep hope alive in her heart.

But time had been against them both. It had been so long since Fowler whisked her newborn child away from her, a child whose father he had beaten so badly that he died. As long as Fowler was the only one who knew the boy's whereabouts, Rita would not rebel. And no one who cared about her was going to kill Fowler, badly as he needed it, when the last hope of finding her and Wad's son would die with him.

He rode steadily west, crossing back over Turkey Neck

and then dropping south along the east margin of Dry Lake to the Split Rock line camp. There was still a light in the dugout that served as quarters, and he hailed the place as he neared it and then rode in.

Frank Landusky and Pete Farraday had been over here with part of the Two C herd since early March and were out of touch. Gila ate a late supper and, meanwhile, brought them up to date.

Landusky was a grizzled man who had helped Chance drive in his first herd of cattle. He sucked on a beat-up pipe while he listened, grimly shaking his head. "So we're outlawed," he commented, finally. "You boys ever had a taste of that? Well, I did, over in Wyoming during some nester trouble. It means we'll be kept out of the general roundup. Can't even send reps to claim our strays, and what this new association picks up in its round it'll impound. That gives a man somethin' to think about, with calf roundup right on top of us."

"After which comes hayin'," Farraday agreed. He was another of the young punchers in the outfit, a short but muscular man who could hold up his end. "What hay outfit wants to contract on a job it might get shot off of? We might get that to do all by ourselves, too."

"Usin' what for machinery?" Landusky growled. "We don't have it and nobody would sell it to a black-listed cow outfit."

"You boys want to throw in your hands?" Gila said testily.

"Who the hell said anything like that?"

They both had bridled, and Gila grinned at them. He could still call himself a young man, but he had ridden enough ranges to know that no ranch was stronger than the individuals who did its work. He didn't see a crack in Two C anywhere, from Chance Abelard down to the horse wrangler.

Gila rolled into a spare bunk when the others turned in, but found himself lying wide awake in the darkness. He and Wad had seen a lot of country together, and he had known him almost as well as he knew himself. Wad had wanted to marry Rita and had hoped for her sake to win her father around first. Rita had said later that he had died without knowing about the baby, or he would have taken her and hit for yonder, come what may.

As it was, Fowler had caught them together and used those powerful shoulders and ironclad fists to settle it the one way he deemed proper. Later he had escaped even being indicted by shamelessly claiming the unwritten law, his right to punish the man who had violated his daughter. Only afterward had he discovered he had destroyed the man who could have spared her unmarried motherhood and would have considered it a privilege to do so.

CHAPTER FIVE

Ren helped Chance into the buggy in which the crippled rancher made occasional inspections of the range, then went around and sprang up on the driver's side. For two steady weeks, warm weather had dried the earth until it was firm enough at last for the vehicle to leave the surfaced roads and lanes and poke off into more remote areas. So Ren wheeled out at once for the western section, between Poison Lake and the Kettle Hills and east of the Indian reserve. The late April sun warmed his back, and his nostrils caught the pleasant aroma of Chance's cigar. Momentarily it was easy to forget that a witches' brew of fury was reaching a boil in the Hard Rock.

The mobile side of Chance's body was toward him, and his face broke in a smile. "Isn't that a magnificent piece of country out there?"

"It sure is," Ren agreed. "But it can get mighty tough at times."

"I like strong country. Don't ask me why." Chance drew on his cigar and fell silent again.

Ren knew what he meant. Before them lay a panorama of desert aridity and green-feathered hills, the latter abruptly breaking the planed smoothness of the basin floor. Off to the northwest he could see streaks of white that marked Poison Lake, a tremendous expanse of cracked and chalky earth. Beyond it, the high desert began to climb away, wheeling to the north, and then off to the east. The sun that struck so pleasantly on their backs was mixing colors off there, soft russets and golds against a horizon of azure mist. Due ahead the flatness simply melted into the sky line, reaching on to the Kettle Plateau and the Indian lands.

They began to see cattle, never more than a few head, and they were the Herefords that Chance had been the first to bring into the Hard Rock. The line riders at Poison Lake kept them under a steady watch and did all the work necessary to take care of them, and these tours of Chance's were little more than excursions he enjoyed, confined as he was so much of the time to his office and house and a sedentary work routine. From time to time Ren reined in to let him soak himself in his surroundings, then the buggy ran on to reach the line camp at noon while the punchers were there.

These were Johnny Harmon and Buck Spalding, who unhitched the team while Ren helped Chance into the shack standing at the edge of the hills, where springs supported a grove of locusts. The two riders had got the noon meal started, and when they came back from the barn Ren realized that something worried them.

"What's wrong, boys?" he said quietly.

Harmon answered. "Well, I rode the reservation side of the range, this morning, and I run into that breed that lives on Wampus Creek. You know him—Cultus Charlie. He told me word's been passed to the Injuns to help themselves to all the Two C beef they can eat. The other outfits won't lift a hand to stop 'em."

Ren's face darkened. "Missed anything?"

"Ain't yet, but we will. Them Injuns don't need a second invite to free beef. We could use a extra man over here, Ren."

"Can't spare one, Johnny," Chance said regretfully. "Just keep your eye peeled. If you see rustling sign, send me word, and I'll take it up with the Indian agent."

"Lot of good that'll do."

"I know. He's probably been warned not to interfere. But

we're over a barrel, boys, thanks to Pearce Jerome and the men who follow his lead. They know Indian rustling won't break us. They're just trying to tie up a few of our men on work that shouldn't be necessary. Just the same, I can't afford to feed Indians free beef, so do the best you can to prevent it."

"Why don't you send off for some hired gunslingers?" Harmon said angrily. "It would save you money in the long run."

Chance looked at him sourly. "At the cost of lives? No, Johnny. Nine tenths of the people bucking us are decent enough. They're just blinded by prejudice and inflamed by haranguing. If they start shooting, we shoot back, but we don't initiate it."

Harmon said reluctantly, "You're right, but it gravels a man to be dogged this way when he's got his hands full of honest work already."

"It'll get worse before it gets better," Ren warned them.

When they had eaten with the line riders, Ren drove his passenger on into the hills, for Chance had wanted to make the ride mainly to check on the summer range himself. A rough, good-weather road ran through the Kettles on the west and south edges of Two C's allotments and came out in the upper end of Crank Creek Valley, making a loop.

They had reached the south edge of the range when Chance said abruptly, "What's that tacked to the tree over there?"

Ren reined in and saw it too, the placard fastened to the bole of a pine on the south side of the narrow road. He dropped to the ground and walked over to the tree. The object of their attention was a printed poster, the ink freshly black, and he read it in mounting anger:

PUBLIC NOTICE

TO WHOM IT MAY CONCERN: Notice is hereby given that Two C Ranch, Chance Abelard, proprietor, having conducted itself in a manner inimical to the public good and disturbing to its peace, has as of this date been outlawed by the below organization, duly constituted under the laws of this state, been expelled from the official roundup district and its crew members black-listed forever. Be it known also that any of its livestock of whatever species found south of this point during general roundup will be impounded and sold, the proceeds going to defray costs. Thereafter, any strays crossing south of this point will be shot on sight.

The deadline officially declared by the below organization and thus legally constituted begins at Needle Point at the edge of the Indian reserve, runs easterly in a straight course to Rooster Head Rock and then in a straight course across North Basin to the headwaters of Deacon Creek on Turkey Neck Ridge.

This action has been taken solely in the interests of the public welfare and peace.

	Cowmen's Protective Association
Alkali, Oregon	Pearce Jerome, President
April 25, 1895	Hugo Patterson, Secretary

Ren ripped the notice from the tree and carried it over to Chance. The rancher read it in silence, his reaction showing only in the bitter glint of his eyes.

"Their declaration of war," Ren said savagely. "We expected everything but the deadline, and they've drawn that way inside our territory. It clips off the edge of our summer grass in the Kettles and on Turkey Head, and it even cuts into our winter range in the basin. Why?"

Chance stared straight ahead, looking old and worn and harried. He said, "We might have put up with it, if they'd set it where our range rightfully ends. They know we won't stand for a thing as outrageous as this."

"That's the way it strikes me. They're making sure we defy it. Surely you can get a court injunction against a thing this highhanded."

Chance shook his head. "There's precedent for what they're doing. Stockmen's associations had the powers of mining districts in the old days, when the law wasn't very well established. Some courts still look at them the same way. Even if I succeeded, they'd counter with a legal move and keep us tied up."

"Which leaves it to Judge Colt."

"Such questions often wind up in his court, I'm afraid."

Ren tossed the notice aside, climbed back to his seat, and drove on. Every mile or so along the arbitrarily set deadline they saw another notice. They didn't bother to destroy them, and in late afternoon arrived at the head of Crank Creek and dropped down into its valley, reaching Two C headquarters at dusk.

The yard buzzed with angry men in from the day's work on the range, for at suppertime Frank Landusky had smoked in from the Split Rock line camp with one of the deadline notices he had found over there. He had brought it to men unaware of the development, and now every ranch hand present wore a look of cold fury. Ren told them he had already seen some of the placards in the Kettles, then he turned the horses over to them and washed up for a belated supper.

Gila followed him into the cookshack. "Whoever's doin' their thinkin'," he said angrily, "is a pure Simple Simon. We'll round up as many of their strays as they will ours. Poorer stock, but it'll sure take the sting outta their damned impounding. Afterward we can shoot anything of theirs that crosses their deadline, coming our way. So what's it gettin' 'em?"

"They know that part's a standoff," Ren said wearily. "They're only after a sure-fire setup for gunplay. I see Link Fowler's hand in that. He must be back from California."

"And getting his next job lined up. Ren, what can we do?"

"Brand our calves, starting as soon as we can get going. Horses ready?"

"All shoed, and the wagon's set."

"Good. We'll start over on the Split Rock range and work north, then swing west to the reservation."

"We're starting at their deadline?"

"At the edge of our actual range."

Gila grinned. "Three-four miles inside their damned line. Fine, and I hope to hell Fowler's there to dispute it."

Ren left headquarters after breakfast, the next morning, and rode out to Bloody Rim to send in the men who had been cutting poles. Afterward he went on to the Dry Gap ranch, but missed Lands, who was still on the high desert with his flocks and herders. He was on the point of heading home to Crank Creek when something that had puzzled him started him off in the opposite direction. Joe Garnet's range was on the Two C side of the deadline, and Ren wondered why the line had not been looped around to divide it from that of the outlawed ranch, also, in keeping with the other outfits. When he saw him last in Alkali, Joe had made it plain that Ren Tyler was no longer a welcome visitor, but Ren set a stubborn course for Marsh Creek.

It did not disappoint him that he failed to reach the ranch during the noon hour for, while her father had already ridden out somewhere on his afternoon rounds, Libby was at the house, giving him a chance to talk with her alone. The clatter of an arriving horse drew her to the door, and her look of mixed pleasure and displeasure was not lost on him. She came on to the edge of the porch as he rode up, standing straight and slender, her fine dark hair pulled back and knotted behind her head. He touched his hat, his face grave with uncertainty. She had not declared any personal hostility, that day in Alkali, yet she had let it be known which side she was on.

"Guess I missed your dad," he said.

"He just left to go up in the hills. Is something wrong?"

Dryly, he said, "Well, there's not an awful lot you could call right, Libby. We've been finding posters plastered along the south side of our range, way over in what's always been acknowledged as our territory. Your father know about them?"

She stared at him somberly, then nodded. "It was all planned at that meeting in town a while back." There was a more open sullenness in her manner than there had been that day, and he could understand why. Like Joe, she was hot-headed and strong feeling, and in spite of Joe's warning he had helped bring sheep into the country, careless of their feelings and his standing with them.

He said, "I guess you figure I had a choice between you and sheep and took sheep. And that we could end all this pronto if we'd just send 'em out of the country and give up. It's not that simple, Libby. I think those flocks're just an excuse somebody's waited for a long while to start big trouble in the Hard Rock. That somebody isn't Pearce Jerome, much as he's always disliked Chance. I think it's Link Fowler. Now that he's got an organization to use and public feeling on his side, he wouldn't quit even if we shot the sheep ourselves and made a public apology."

He knew immediately that he had touched upon something that lay unspoken in her mind. Her troubled eyes glanced suddenly away, and then she confused him by looking back in stony impassivity. "You're very glib, but you haven't changed the fact that Two C asked for what's being done in an effort to make it act like a civilized ranch again."

"All right, Libby. What I come over about's calf roundup. Since we've got to conduct our own, we're starting early—tomorrow or the day after. I aim to send your strays home to you. Does Joe intend to let the association impound such of ours as is found on his range?"

Her head came up, and her eyes were openly angry. "Do you expect him to fight the association, when he's utterly out of sympathy with you?"

"Fight 'em? That sounds like he's being coerced." Ren was glad she had let that slip, for it was his hunch that Joe wouldn't stand for a deadline between his spread and Two C, a sure way to carry the two outfits on into bloody conflict. "Tell him what I said about his strays."

"I will."

He touched his hat and rode off.

He hadn't even been asked to light down where once, at this time of day, he would have been asked if he had eaten lately, and if he hadn't Libby would have insisted on feeding him. On a warm day like this, there would at least have been lemonade and cookies, maybe cake, the little things women like to do for men they care about. Well, there would be no more of that, and he couldn't blame her. He had paid unhurried court, horning other suitors out, letting her draw her natural conclusions. Then without a by-your-leave he had thrown away his future, never realizing that this involved her future, too, if she was feeling the way he hoped. When she had no more sympathy for his actions than if he had started robbing banks, she had reason to be deeply hurt.

CHAPTER SIX

From the rim above Marsh Creek, Link Fowler saw the horseman ride away from Garnet's house, and his spyglasses soon showed him that it was Ren Tyler. Garnet's girl stood motionless in the yard for long moments afterward, watching in the direction Ren had taken, and Fowler kept the glasses on her. Small as her image was, it had those exciting lines that, with her youngness, had always heated him privately. It was obvious that the girl below was smitten on the man now receding in the distance, and he felt again the overpowering hostility Tyler always stirred in him.

"What's so interestin'?" Hunk Roddy said at his elbow.

"That's just a filly worth lookin' at. Let's go down and see what kind of truck she was having with Ren Tyler."

Roddy's face darkened. "So that was Tyler." He had not forgotten the three days he had been held prisoner.

"Nobody else."

They rode back to the head of a shelf road that would let them down to the creek bottom, not hurrying the tired horses that had that day carried them onto the high desert for a look at Abelard's sheep. Accustomed as they were to sneaking in on wild horses, they had been unable to get anywhere near the flocks without arousing dogs that promptly betrayed their presence to equally alert and rifle-packing herders. That had been a surprise to Fowler, informing him that the creatures and their despised guardians were not as vulnerable as he had supposed, and he had postponed his intention of making a little trouble to get even for his stampeded horses.

They came out presently on the creek bottom and struck across to the Garnet house. Libby had gone back indoors, but she reappeared when they rode into the yard, and Fowler was not flattered by the uneasiness that came quickly into her face. He rode up to the edge of the porch, Roddy tagging him, and their dust rolled on toward her.

"Howdy, Libby," Fowler said with emphasized cordiality. "I take it from the empty corral that Joe's off someplace."

She nodded reluctantly, not liking to admit she was the only one there. Fowler scarcely blamed her, knowing that he was a pretty rough-looking customer. And there weren't many women in the Hard Rock who cared to be caught alone by Roddy.

"Seen a man ridin' off on a Two C horse," Fowler continued, "so we figured we'd better see if one of them hooligans had bothered you."

"Of course not," she said, openly irritated. "That was Ren Tyler."

"Ren? What was he after?"

"Nothing but to tell my father they're starting to brand calves in a day or two."

Fowler straightened. "So soon? He say where they're starting?"

She shook her head, and he had a feeling she wouldn't divulge it even if she had been told.

She intrigued and maddened Fowler, and someday he would see how far he could go with her. The aloofness and ladylike ways didn't impress him. Women were all the same underneath, susceptible to a real he-man. Already she had pinked under his inspection, compelled by it to realize her weaknesses.

"Well," Fowler said, "it was mighty nice of him to let you know. Why?"

"He wanted to know if Dad would follow the association rule about strays."

"What did you tell him?"

"That I don't know." Her head came up. "Look here, Link Fowler. What business have you got to question me? Are you running the association?"

He laughed. "Don't get your hackles up, Libby. We've got that outfit cornered, and it's a good idea to watch it, that's all."

Hotly, she said, "Cornered? Is that the way you had Ren at Massacre Pass?"

Stung by the reminder, he said roughly, "You're really gone on the galoot, ain't you?"

"That's none of your business." She turned and fled into the house.

"Let me teach her a lesson," Roddy muttered.

"When I'm ready, I'll do the teachin'."

They struck east toward Turkey Neck, which they had only to cross to come down in the east basin and his range that ran along the lake marshes and up Deacon Creek to the ridge.

"So she wanted to know if I'm runnin' things," Fowler mused. "Well, there'll be others with the same wonder before the dust's settled."

"Then they won't wonder," Roddy agreed. "They'll know."

"If Lady Luck keeps smilin' the way she's been."

Fowler had more respect for that mythical female than for any of her flesh-and-blood counterparts, and lately he had seemed much in her favor in spite of the setback at the pass. The luck began in California when he got wind of the sheep Abelard had bought. By the time he reached home with the news, he had known that he had a hold on something that could mean much to him personally, a way to control the

most powerful man in the Hard Rock, his neighbor, Pearce
Jerome. And the old mossy-horn had jumped at the chance
to release his jealous hatred of Chance Abelard under the
cover of a just cause. He didn't realize yet that his own
throat had already been cut. For Fowler meant to run things,
to work his way into a control of the association so powerful
he could turn it against its own members if any of them
balked. Then he aimed to spread himself westward, picking
off the range of Varley Eden and Joe Garnet and finally of
Two C, itself, to shape up the finest horse ranch a man could
imagine.

They topped the ridge to see East Basin wheel below them
in soft blue light, then Fowler spurred his horse down the
long grade, leaving it to Roddy to keep up or fall behind,
and presently came to his headquarters. Racket and dust
carried from the traps where his men were topping out the
last catch of wildlings he would take from the breaks for a
while, for through the next weeks he wanted his crew on
hand to carry out such purposes as events inspired.

He liked the savagery of the quick and vicious breaking
he gave his mustangs, although he sold them in distant mar-
kets for thoroughly gentled horses, and while he and Roddy
unsaddled he listened with satisfaction to the grunts and
squeals and sudden hammering tattoos of hoofs, with now
and then a crash when some heavy body hit a fence. Then
he walked silently with his foreman to the house for the
midday meal that they had been obliged to postpone a few
hours.

He didn't announce their presence or requirement to Rita,
but she heard them and looked out the door. She knew by
the way they stopped at the pump to wash that they were
hungry, and she was used to his sudden and surly demands
for food at any hour. It had been kept warm from the noon
meal and was on the table when Fowler came into the house.

Again no word passed between the girl and the men, who sat down to eat with wolfish speed and appetite.

Roddy finished first and went out to join the men at the breaking pens. Fowler remained at the table and rolled a cigarette, his eyes on his daughter. She had always been sullen and silent with him, which seemed only to sharpen his awareness of how shapely and pretty she was. He would never forgive her for her misconduct with the drifter he had hired that summer, a few years back, nor would he ever tell her what he had done with the get from it.

When her voice shattered the brooding silence, it startled Fowler. "If you don't get rid of that Meathead," she said, "I'm going to kill him."

He blinked his eyes. "Meathead? He been givin' you trouble?"

"Well, you leave me here alone with him once more, and you'll find him dead."

Fowler kept staring at her. Meathead? The half-wit was the one man on the spread he had thought he could trust with her, but even simpletons could get frisky ideas, apparently. "He harmed you?" he said, and was surprised at the raggedness of his voice.

She looked at him a long moment, maybe understanding his jealousy and the jealousy he still felt for Wad Wadsworth. "Just get rid of him. I don't need any watchdog. You know I'll never leave without you telling me what happened to my baby."

"Mebbe not," he agreed. "But how about the fancy Dans that'd be pawin' around you if somebody wasn't on hand to drive 'em off?"

She stared at him with dull eyes. "Is it just me, or do you think all women are rutting bitches?"

"Who showed me what you are?" he snapped.

He wondered if she was lying about Meathead, hoping to get rid of him so she could be left alone here now and then, so she could entertain some sneaking outsider. That could well be, but on the other hand he wasn't having the half-wit lusting after her, even if it went no further than that. He didn't say anything more to her, but when he went out to the corrals and saw Meathead helping the peelers, he made up his mind. Even though he had no brain, the young giant was like a magnificent stallion in physique. Maybe Rita was the one getting the ideas and wanted to remove the temptation because of what had happened after the other man bewitched her.

Moreover, Fowler reflected in a sudden uplifting discernment, Meathead could be just what he needed to further his intentions.

He didn't speak to the big fellow, going on instead to catch a fresh horse and saddle it. Afterward he rode south toward Crown, timing his gait to get there around suppertime, when he could be sure old Pearce would be at headquarters.

Pearce Jerome had picked off the prime land in the Hard Rock when he moved into it so long ago and drove out the Indians, a conquest he still bragged about and took for proof of his right to rule the country, and which made him so touchy of Chance Abelard's knack for leadership. On Fowler's right ran the interconnected lakes that absorbed the runoff of the east basin and, bordering them, the wide marshlands that Jerome refused to touch, even though he could do even more in that respect than Abelard had done if he was less stubborn. Beyond the lakes and hazy in the distance were the Wildhorse breaks, which Fowler knew as he knew his own dooryard. But he was through with mustanging, much as he liked the chase. Presently he'd be doing nothing but raising and training blooded horses for the luxury market.

He topped the last rise before Crown headquarters to see Jerome, himself, riding in from some point on the westward ridge. Fowler reined in to wait for him, meanwhile studying the most baronial ranch layout in the Hard Rock with the idea of equaling or bettering it one day himself. The buildings were spread below him where Juniper Creek broadened into a lagoon before losing itself in the marsh. Poplars, cottonwoods, and locusts shaded them, and the complex suggested a much more prosperous ranch than the big Crown had been for a long while. Fowler agreed with those who said Jerome's big trouble was his refusal to keep up with the times. But long ago he had got on Jerome's good side by lambasting the newfangled and ridiculing the Johnny-come-latelies when he was around the man.

"Howdy, Pearce," Fowler said with cheerful familiarity, when Jerome rode up and reined in. "Me and the boys put up the posters along the deadline. Two C knows about it, and we'll soon know what they're gonna do about it. I just heard they're startin' to brand calves in a day or so."

"Yeah," Jerome said, his eyes glinting. "But don't forget, Link. They've got a right to round up on their side of the deadline. That's why we moved it in on 'em so far they're bound to cross. You see that whatever happens is on our side, with them out of bounds. Some of the outfits don't like the idea of giving you so much rope when we're on shaky legal ground already."

It was no secret to Fowler that he wasn't the most popular man in the basin, which bothered him and had influenced his actions. He had to pull the association behind him solidly, get it to accept his and not Jerome's leadership, and that meant he had to arouse its sympathy.

He said, "Look, Pearce. What you want is to bring Chance Abelard to his knees. Right? And you want to do it in a way that'll make it look like his own damned fault. All right. You play that game, and let me play mine."

Jerome eyed him. "Don't reckon I get you."

"You're trying to squeeze Abelard so hard he'll go as bronco as you're making out he is already. Your black list and deadline might do it—in time. You run that end. Then you'll know you're nice and safe with public feeling. I've got my own squabble, considerin' what Tyler did to my horse drive. I'll go on from there on my own hook."

"You get too rough, and we'll disown you completely."

Fowler laughed. "Want to bet you don't start backin' me to the hilt? You and all the other outfits so exercised over the sheep."

After a moment's thought, Jerome said, "Don't know what you're drivin' at, and mebbe I don't want to. But it's like somebody seems to have told the reserve Injuns. None of us is gonna get exercised over Abelard's troubles, no matter what. We just don't want anything too raw charged to us."

They separated, Fowler riding north again, gratified. The old man had given him a free hand, without really saying so, and assurance that the association would not interfere with him while withholding its official backing. That was all the agreement he needed at present, for he didn't want to have to clear everything he did with somebody else. If things went right, it would be too fast and furious for that.

Across the distance he could see Jerome's riders, singly and in pairs, heading in for their suppers and a night's rest. He was in no hurry for his own meal, having eaten in mid-afternoon, and when finally no one was visible he angled his horse ridgeward toward the Deacon Creek pass. A soft dusk had settled when he reached the ridge and struck onto it, coming in among the juniper and scattered pine. Thereafter he sat his horse in slack comfort while it took him down the plateau that bottomed on the rim above Two C's Split Rock line camp.

Night had clamped down by the time he halted atop the bluff that sharply separated the floor of the basin from the hills of Turkey Ridge. Well out in the distance was the white mineral bed of Dry Lake, grown luminescent in the last light, but his attention was centered on the nearer cow camp.

It disclosed an extraordinary number of men and horses, and he saw a wagon's dim shape over by the pole stable. He smiled softly into the growing darkness. Two C was starting its gather at this point, he realized, its crew stripped to supply the manpower for it. That meant none of its riders would be ramming around on the loose for quite a while. It was what he had wanted to be sure of and, swinging his horse, he slipped away and let the full night swallow him.

When he reached home he went immediately to the bunkhouse, where Roddy had drawn everyone but Meathead into a card game. The giant sat on his bunk, braiding a lariat from horsehair he had gathered with infinite patience. Fowler wanted witnesses to what he had to say to him, but that was as much as he wanted even his men to know of his plans. The card game halted when he entered the smoky, lamplighted room, the players looking up at him. He ignored them.

"Meathead," he said, with the rough affection he sometimes showed the nitwit, "get you an early breakfast in the morning, then hit the saddle for that hardscrabble cow outfit up by Cottonwood Buttes. Tell 'em I've got a few broomtails I'll sell dirt cheap, if they're in the market. Then you get back here, you understand, and don't go galavantin' around playin' Injun."

Meathead stared at him sullenly, but Fowler knew he understood the instructions and would follow them precisely. The little Cottonwood outfit was on the high desert, so poor that when it needed to buy another horse or so it bought culls from Fowler. The trail would take Meathead past the sheep flock Fowler had checked that morning with Roddy, and his Indianlike curiosity would compel him to stop for a look-see. That was all Fowler wanted of him.

Turning to Roddy, Fowler said, "You and the boys keep after the stuff in the pens. I'm gonna be gone most of tomorrow. I've been hankerin' to see if anything worth trapping's drifted into the breaks."

Surprised, Roddy said, "Thought we weren't gonna go after any more for a while."

Fowler grinned at him. "It's like a tosspot tryin' to go on the wagon for a old hand like me to give up the 'stangs entirely."

CHAPTER SEVEN

The scarlet edge of day showed above Turkey Neck when Ren settled his feet in his boots and took a sleepy look at the awakening camp. He had stripped the ranch to a skeleton crew in throwing together this branding outfit, which now stirred about him or still sat on bedrolls getting into clothes. The nighthawk had brought in the horses, and Abe Jewett had breakfast ready. He had cooked over a fire pit over by the springs, for the line shack's stove was much too small for feeding a contingent this size.

Gila Veyan came toward him from the springs, where he had washed his face and combed his hair, and he was rolling a smoke while he walked. Ren picked up a towel and bar of soap and headed for the springs, but Gila stopped him where they met.

"Well," Gila drawled, "today ought to show us how much they mean it."

"Their deadline? They mean it."

"But how far are they ready to go to make it stick? Old Pearce must know he's on shaky ground, so mebbe he's only bluffing."

"Hope so, but I wouldn't bank on it."

"Who's goin' to work the far side of it?"

"You and me and somebody else who can keep his head. Maybe Frank Landusky."

Gila grinned thinly and went on to the fire to badger old

Abe, who wasn't too happy about being appointed roundup cook. Proceeding to the tank below the springs, Ren washed up, thinking of the coming day. Then he heard the cook's brayed summons and joined the men for breakfast.

Afterward he went over to the *remuda* and roped the horse he would ride that morning; most of the circle riders were on hand there already and saddling up. He told them that the roundup ground, the central point to which the cattle they gathered that morning would be driven, was Squaw Belly Rock, on Two C's side of the deadline. Then he led his horse over to the cook fire and told the jingler the same thing and ordered him to have the *remuda*, branding equipment, and cold lunches at Squaw Belly at noon.

He led the men on a sharp slant up the ridge and near the summit swung them south, moving swiftly and dropping off a rider about once a mile. The first ones would wait in place until those with farther to travel were set. Then they would all start in at about the same time, scouring the plateau and its countless hiding places, and sweeping cattle and calves toward Squaw Belly. He didn't make a show of picking anyone to go over the deadline with him and Gila, but when they reached it Frank Landusky was the only one left with them, and that was not by chance.

Gila pointed to an association poster tacked to a pine, saying, "Here's their high and mighty stop line. So do we stop and let the horses decorate it for them with some droppings?"

Dryly, Ren said, "We don't respect it even that much."

A mile past that point he dropped off Landusky, knowing the puncher's cool courage was balanced by a wise head. He and Gila descended rapidly thereafter, Gila stopping midway down the slope and Ren going on to the flat below. They were dangerously past the imperiously set limit by then, and it would take a couple of hours to work the country and get back on undisputed ground. He had no personal fear of what the association might do, but he had the lives of his men to consider and important work to accomplish.

He started in immediately, covering the flat strip next to the dry lake, shoving ahead of him everything he saw that could walk, poking into hidden spots, and snaking slowly in the direction of Squaw Belly. Frequently he stopped for a look to rearward, only to find himself the only human being in the area. When presently he threw the last steer over the line, he was as puzzled as relieved that no one from the association had put in an appearance. At the very least, he had expected to see something of Link Fowler.

Soon afterward his drive closed with Gila's, and shortly they picked up Landusky, and neither man had seen anyone to dispute their starting their supposedly outlawed roundup where they had.

"Looks like nobody realized we're startin' ahead of schedule," Gila reflected.

"I told Joe Garnet," Ren said. "That is, Libby, and she'd tell him."

"Well, Joe's one man who won't bust a gut to give us trouble, even if he is on the other side of this argument."

"I hope you're right," Ren agreed. "It could be he didn't pass the word along."

"That, or I was right about them bluffing."

By noon the first roundup had been thrown together at Squaw Belly, drawn from a dozen different compass points. The jingler had brought down the *remuda* and tools, with coffee and cold steak sandwiches that the punchers put away with dispatch. By then the herd had simmered down from the excitement of the drive, and the riders mounted fresh horses and started to cut it, throwing the strays to one side and the cows with calves to the other.

Ren was tallying when, around two o'clock, a rider came whipping along the lake margin from the north. They had started to brand, and Gila was roping. Having just hauled a bawling calf to the fire, Gila paused to take his own look at the dust-lifting oncomer, his attention directed by Ren's stare. Then he rode over to Ren.

"That's Lands' cayuse," he said.

"It sure is," Ren agreed. "Mebbe with the answer to why we weren't given any trouble when we went over the deadline."

"Lands caught it, instead of us?"

"Something's sure got him coverin' ground."

Yancy Lands had been a cowpuncher and knew better than to run his horse too close to the cattle. He slowed and came in at a walk, but was plainly impatient. His face confirmed the impression that something concerned him deeply.

"What's up, Yancy?" Ren said.

"Sure wish I knew," Lands said on a heavy expulsion of breath. "Knew why, that is. We found a dead man this morning, up by the east flock."

"A herder?" Ren said sharply.

Lands shook his head. "No, thank God. Hard to say what he was, though the body's range-dressed. A moose of a fella, and hardly more'n a kid. Ben and Si's with that band, and they heard a shot around nine this mornin'. Wouldn't have thought much of it except the dogs acted funny. When they looked around they found this fella. Shot in the back with a rifle. He'd been forkin' a pinto, which hadn't strayed far off."

"Big man—pinto—?" Gila said. "Ren, that's Meathead—you know—the dumb cluck that works for Fowler."

"Worked," Lands corrected. "Fowler's the hombre that tried to make trouble at the pass, ain't he?"

Ren nodded. "Meathead strayed into this country several years ago, just a kid but way overgrown and not bright. Stumbled into Fowler's mustang camp, and Link took a twisted shine to him. Meathead's been with the outfit ever since, and he'd do anything Link told him to."

"You mean Link might have sent him to plague the sheep?" Gila asked.

"Don't know what with," Lands said. "He didn't have a gun with him. But that ain't what you're driving at, Ren."

"No," Ren admitted. "Whatever took him there, Meathead was close to the sheep. The herders could have killed him, and they can't prove they didn't, can they?"

Lands shook his head. "They didn't shoot, but there's nothing but their word for it. We covered the body and left it right where the boys found it. I want the sheriff to see for himself."

"And I want a look. You take over here, Gila, and send Frank to Alkali for the sheriff. Tell him not to talk about it to anybody else. Yancy and me'll go back up with the flocks."

"Expect more trouble up there?" Gila said.

"When word gets around the kid was killed by a sheep-herder, which'll be the claim, we're gonna catch it like we never expected."

"Who did kill him?"

"It's a safe bet it was somebody who wants this squabble hotter and bloodier than it's been so far. A man that twisted could send Meathead there and then back-shoot him himself."

Bitterly, Gila said, "You're describing Fowler."

"Don't Rita prove it?"

"She sure does."

"But *we* can't prove it, and before we'll get a chance we'll have bally hell on our hands."

Gila whistled. "Man, have we been boxed? Rustlers from the reserve to guard against, a deadline to keep our strays from crossing if we don't want 'em shot, and now sheep again. West, south, and north. Wonder what'll happen on our east side?"

While Lands ate a quick meal, Ren saddled fresh mounts from the horse band. Afterward they struck out, and in about two hours passed Joe Garnet's place on Marsh Creek at too

great a distance to see anybody. Soon they were climbing to
the high desert, but, swiftly as they traveled, there was barely
enough light left to study the scene of the killing when they
reached it.

This flock was feeding in an area of open slope whose
wheeling distances were broken only in places where rock
crops and gully washes relieved the monotony. The body lay
in the shade of an overgrown sage clump under a piece of
canvas, moved only a short distance from where it had been
found in order to protect it from the beating desert sun. The
bullet that had killed the young giant had drilled its lethal
tunnel between the shoulder blades, and it had gone into the
heart.

Ren had Si Botwood show him the position of the body
when found, which failed to help him form a picture of what
had happened. Meathead had been aboard the broken mustang when hit, and the animal had wheeled and sprung away
from the spot before it dumped him. So, Lands helping,
Ren scouted until they picked up Meathead's trail coming
in on the sheep, and they followed it to where Lands said
the flock had been at that time. Ren sat his horse in Meathead's probable position when he did his spying, then turned
and took a look behind him.

There were two places where the killer could have slipped
in behind him close enough for an effective shot. Meathead
had a reputation for unusually keen senses, but the constant
blatting of the flock would cover the sound of the killer's
movements. Ren rode back to one place, a rock scab, but
found no horse or boot tracks. Then he went over to a low
hummock, and there he found what he hunted.

A horse had stopped here long enough to impress several
prints on the loose soil, then it had swung and moved slowly
eastward. Keeping to the side, Ren followed the trail for
nearly a mile. At that point the mysterious horseman had
ridden into a creek, suggesting that he was experienced in

furtiveness. He could have gone upstream or down and would have stayed in the water for miles, so there was little chance of picking up his tracks again before the plateau wind rubbed them out.

The dusk was deep when finally Ren rode in to the sheep camp with Lands. More than once, since he came in contact with these people, he had marveled at the compact efficiency of a sheep wagon and the economy of effort with which the herders controlled the several thousand creatures in their charge and turned them into that many small factories producing wool and lambs. The canvas-covered wagon held a stove, table, and bed, with storage space for a surprising amount of equipment and provisions. Even so, the quarters were too cramped for five men, and they ate their late supper outdoors.

"How long'll it take for the lawman to get here?" Botwood said troubledly.

"Depends on whether my rider can find him. If he can't, God knows when. If he's lucky, they could cut it by daylight."

"What sort of a jigger is he?"

Ren sighed. "I wish he was a little less the typical cowtowner. He's honest, but he's got a lot of association friends, to say nothing of the fact that they voted him into office."

"He sure ain't got enough to stick this killin' on me and Ben."

"He'll have so much heat on him," Ren said candidly, "he's gonna try. It's got me worried, boys, and you might as well know it's gonna be rough for you."

He knew that meant for himself, as well. The crime obviously had been framed to incriminate the sheepmen, but he found it hard to accept that Jerome, for all his intemperate views, would authorize anything so cold-blooded. Someone else, and his mind went unerringly to Link Fowler again, was playing an obscure part in the range war for an equally mysterious stake. That bode ill for everyone concerned, for they were all being made cat's-paws in a thoroughly vicious and wholly inscrutable plot.

The night deepened, and stars came over the desert in a million burning pricks in the sky. The scent-laden wind lisped through the sage and was rubbing away the few horse tracks that hinted at the true story of the killing. Then, just as they were fixing to bed down, the dogs began to worry, and the men swung to stare into the sweeping darkness to the south.

"Hossbackers," Lands said to Ren, "and it's too soon for your man and the sheriff. Ben, you and Si take your rifles and get in the wagon till we know what's up."

"Mebbe," Botwood said nervously, "they're aimin' at the band."

"Makin' too much noise. They're coming to the camp."

Five minutes passed before a party of three men appeared in the benighted distance, slowed to a trot but riding steadily toward the fire. Ren and Lands stood watching them closely.

In a moment, Ren said, "It's Fowler and a couple of his mustangers."

"The boys in the wagon'll cover 'em," Lands assured him.

Fowler was accompanied by Hunk Roddy and a man Ren had seen before but did not know. They pulled up at the edge of the firelight, and Fowler took a long look at the two men who stood there in silent watchfulness. Then the mustanger spoke in an unexpectedly mild manner.

"You fellas see a man of mine along here, today?"

"Like what man?" Ren answered.

"That kid Meathead. I sent him up to Cottonwood Buttes about some horses, this morning. He ought to've got home a long time ago, but he ain't showed. He'd've went past here, so I figured I'd better check with you."

"We seen him, Link," Ren said. "You know that. Also that he's dead."

"Dead?"

Ren would have sworn that Roddy and the other man, at least, were dumfounded.

"Meathead's dead?" Fowler resumed. "You tryin' to get funny?"

"Cut it out, Link. Somebody bushwhacked Meathead down the slope a piece, early this morning. Shot him in the back. Rigging it to look like the sheepers done it."

"What kind of wild yarn is this?" Hunk Roddy said furiously. The third man shared his look of utter incredulity.

"Meathead's dead. Beefed by a drygulcher's slug."

"We'll believe that when we see the carcass," Fowler retorted. "Where is it, if you ain't lyin'?"

"It's waitin' for the sheriff to have a good look in the morning. He's sent for, and there's nothing you can do except mebbe foul the sign. Is that one of the reasons you come up here?"

In a bawling voice, Fowler said, "So that's it. You killed him, and you're trying to let on I did. How crazy can you get? That kid was stupid, but he was like my own boy. By God, we're takin' over here till we see what's goin' on." His hand made a slap that brought up the six-gun from his hip. It was the swift, clean draw of a man who knew he had left many enemies on his back trail and knew he might face retribution at any time. Not until he had covered the two standing men did his companions find courage to fist their own weapons.

"Put 'em away, gents," Lands said mildly, "and take a look at that wagon."

The mustangers' eyes trailed to the sheep wagon, for the first time seeing the ends of two rifle barrels showing through the slits in the canvas. They settled their weapons back in the leather as quickly as they had plucked them. The firelight heightened the outrage streaking the eyes of Roddy and the nameless man, and Ren thought: If Fowler's guilty, they don't know about it, and it looks like they had a sort of fondness for the kid themselves.

"Don't go off half cocked, Hunk," he warned. "This is what happened. This morning the herders with this sheep band heard a rifle shot over east. The dogs stayed uneasy, so they took a look and found the kid and that pinto he rode. He'd been shot from the ridge behind him while he was taking a look at the sheep. Shot in the back, mind you, and I've got a hunch Link knew that when he brought you up here."

"I reckon it was like you say," Roddy retorted, "except he was shot by one of your sheepers. That kid was just curious. He never toted a hog-leg in his life. And if he was shot in the back, he was only trying to get away from you."

Turning to Fowler, Ren said, "You'd better hit for home, Link. When the sheriff's done with Meathead's body, you can have it. Till then, keep out of it."

"You'll pay for it, by God. I'll see you do."

Fowler punctuated the threat with a brittle stare, then he swung his horse and rode off, towing his men behind him.

CHAPTER EIGHT

It was midmorning before Mack Shadel, the sheriff, put in an appearance, and, watching from the camp, Ren climbed the sheep-wagon steps for a long, hard look at the large aggregation of riders coming up the slope. There seemed to be at least twenty of them, compactly grouped and lending the impression of a hostile army. When he saw the stallion one of them rode, he understood it better.

"Thought your man wasn't to breeze it around," Lands said uneasily. "Or is your sheriff mouthy?"

"It wasn't Landusky who spread it," Ren answered. "Or the sheriff. It was Fowler. That's him on the stallion."

"Think he recruited a necktie party?"

"No, I think that big fella next to him's Sheriff Shadel. He wouldn't stand for that."

"If he can keep 'em in hand."

"That's right. I'll meet 'em down by the body. No use in you boys mixin' with 'em unless you have to. Shadel'll have questions, but I'll try and get him up here alone."

Walking down to where Meathead lay, Ren came close enough to identify not only the sheriff, Fowler, and Pearce Jerome, but Bid Warren, the veterinary who was also county coroner, and he felt apprehension riffle through his nervous system when his impression was confirmed that the rest were Fowler and Jerome hirlings. Whether or not Jerome was in on it, Fowler had something going that had to be countered, and it was like trying to fight a man while blind-folded.

When they came up to where he stood, he said curtly to the sheriff, "Why the army, Mack? Or did you swear 'em in as a posse?"

"They come on their own hook," Shadel snapped. He was a big man, rough and blunt of manner, but he took his duties seriously and tried to perform them justly. Yet it was not hard to guess where his sympathies lay, for he had been a cowman before elected to his office. He swung down, walked to the body, and pulled off the tarp covering it. "That's the maverick kid, all right," he said to Bid Warren, who nodded. "Clear case of murder, whoever done it. Don't reckon there's need for an inquest."

Warren, a gaunt, stooped, and gray man, knew more about the livestock he doctored than he did about people. He looked inadequate and plainly was uneasy in the presence of the hostile riders who watched them. They turned the body over and saw where the bullet had drilled in between the shoulder blades. Shadel straightened and looked around, rubbing his hand over his mouth.

"How was he layin' when found?" he said, casting a pene-trating look at Ren.

"He was mounted, and the horse frisked at the shot and dumped him. So that showed nothing about where the killer was. But before dark last night there were horse tracks just past that rise over there. Somebody followed him and waited there to get a good shot."

"Let's have a look."

The others started to follow, but the sheriff told them to stay put, and Ren walked along with him in growing dismay. The party had ridden right over the spot where he had found the telltale sign, which may or not have been by accident.

When they reached the crest, he said, "No use. It was right there in the center of your own tracks. I'm not tryin' to do your work for you, Mack, and I know how you probably feel. But this isn't what it's supposed to look like. Just keep your mind open to that possibility, will you?"

Sourly, Shadel said, "You know what'll happen to them two herders if I don't take 'em in? They'll be strung up without a trial."

"That wouldn't be as easy as you seem to figure. Aren't you going to hear their version?"

"Reckon I'll ask some questions. But I'm warning you. They've got no witnesses, and their word ain't worth a hoot."

"What's their motive?"

"They don't like a cowman, which they probably mistook the kid to be. And when it comes to that, who else had anything against Meathead? Most folks were kind of sorry for him."

"Like Fowler, who took him in?" Ren said softly. "I don't think dislike or a grudge had anything to do with it, Mack. I think he was simply used by somebody who wants more done to Two C than the association's done so far."

"Like old Pearce?" Shadel was openly disdainful. "He's the only man I know who ever really hated Chance Abelard before this sheep business. You tryin' to get my loop on him?"

"I don't think Pearce would go that far. I'm not trying to turn your suspicions to anybody. That's your job, just as it's mine to stand up for the men workin' for my outfit. The most I can do that way right now is get you to see there might be more to this than meets the eye."

"Well, maybe," Shadel admitted. "There ain't much to go on either way, but I do know this. There'll be more law and order around if I take them herders in and lock 'em up for a hearing than if I let 'em run loose while I gather evidence."

"You think your armed escort'd ever let you get to Alkali with 'em?"

"They better."

"When'd they get a hearing?"

"Next court session."

"No bail?"

"Not on first-degree murder."

They stepped wide of the waiting riders in going down to the camp, but this was too much for Shadel's self-appointed assistants, and they followed. Lands, Si Botwood, and Ben Corbett stood there at the sheep wagon, grim-featured but steady-eyed. Under Shadel's questioning the herders told precisely the same story they had told Ren. Their only connection with Meathead's death had come after they heard a shot and their dogs kept acting uneasy. Then they had only found the body and moved it out of the hot sun and covered it as an act of decency.

"Sure," Fowler broke in angrily. "Also tryin' to cover their tracks, Shadel. Anybody can see that."

A murmur of agreement raveled through the mustangers and Crown men, and Ren sensed the highly unstable danger in them. Shadel was sound in his worry as to what they would do unless he made arrests here and now.

"If you're through questionin' my men, Sheriff," he said, "have you asked Fowler how Meathead happened to be here?"

"I told him," Fowler snapped.

"You asked what him and his men were doing at the time Meathead was killed?"

"Where do you get off askin' questions?" Fowler demanded.

Shadel looked at him thoughtfully. "I understand your feelings, Link, seeing how you took care of the kid. But we've got to have impartial facts, so I'll ask the same thing."

"Hunk there," Fowler said, with a nod at Roddy, "had the boys in the traps breakin' the last of a batch of broomies. They were at it all that day. Me, I went up into the breaks to see if I could spot anythin' worth catching. Gone nearly all day. Come back to hear Meathead hadn't showed back from his errand and got worried about him."

"Anybody go with you into the breaks?"

"Hell, Mack, I been workin' them for years. Think I need a escort?"

"You can't prove you didn't follow Meathead?"

"Why in blazes would I?"

"How come you killed another man who worked for you?" Ren said softly. "Namely Wad Wadsworth."

That had been a shot in the dark, and the reaction in Fowler surprised even his own men. A blind fury gathered in his face, and the veins swelled. "Don't bring my young 'un into this!" he shouted. "Damn you, Tyler, I'll drive your teeth down your throat!"

"Nobody mentioned her, Link," Ren's mild voice taunted. "What's the matter? What made *you* bring her up?"

In the hushed immobility of the watchers, Fowler's breathing was noisy although he was trying to get hold of himself. Hunk Roddy in particular was eying him intently, and Pearce Jerome looked startled and bewildered. Mack Shadel rubbed his mouth and shifted his weight on his feet.

The sheriff said, "Simmer down, Link. I'm arrestin' these two sheepherders for the murder. Personally, I only questioned you to show Pearce, here, there's two sides to the coin, that it could have been somebody else. I never said so, and I don't think so, but I want to get my prisoners to town safe and sound for a legal trial. I know you and your boys're plenty worked up about Meathead and might get ideas, but I don't think Pearce'd let you take things in your own hands as long as I'm doin' my job. That right, Pearce?"

Jerome seemed of two minds about that, but Shadel had boxed him neatly. He was head of the new association and as such could hardly risk open defiance and disrespect for the law.

"Arrest 'em," he growled, "and they'll get to Alkali."

Lands was scowling, but he understood as Ren did that Shadel's move was best for his men. Botwood and Corbett liked it even less, but when Lands nodded at them, they said nothing in protest.

"It gives us time to dig into the truth," Ren told the sheepherders openly. "And you can count on us doing our damnedest."

"Better'n a necktie party, I reckon," Botwood muttered. "But not much."

Ten minutes later Ren found himself alone at the camp with Lands while the visitors, carrying the body and escorting the prisoners, faded into the distance. Then Ren poured a cup of coffee, rolled and lighted a cigarette, feeling depressed.

"You hit a mighty touchy nerve in Fowler," Lands commented. "Have a reason?"

"Played a hunch." Ren told him about Wad and Rita and their child who—if still alive—had been separated from its mother almost from its birth. "It's just that he's touchy about that, I reckon. He knows how this country's always felt."

"Yet Meathead could've got interested in the girl."

"At least it makes a motive for Fowler's killing him the basin'd be more willing to accept than my notion he only wants to stir up hotter feelings than Chance did when he brought in the sheep."

"Maybe he wanted to get rid of the kid and saw how to do both at once."

"That's what I'm wondering, and it would be typical of Link."

"So far he's succeeded," Lands reflected. "The case against Si and Ben's so farfetched, my men are going to be mighty hot under the collar."

Ren nodded. "My men'll be harder to handle after this, too. Not that they've come to love a sheepherder. They're gettin' tired of their outfit stoppin' all the punches without throwin' a few."

"Well, I'm going to be stretched thin with them two rotting

in jail. I'll have to go down to Gap Ranch and take a couple of boys off the work there."

"I've got to tell Chance about this, so why don't you stay with the sheep and let me stop at the gap? Who do you want?"

"Any two. All my herders're good ones."

Ren stopped at Dry Gap to send the men to Lands, and then headed west to the home ranch, where he told Chance what had happened on the high desert.

"Holding them without a formal hearing and charge?" Chance said angrily. "They can't do that. I'll send outside for the best damned lawyer I can hire and get 'em out on a writ of habeas corpus."

"Don't think I would, Chance," Ren said with a shake of the head.

"Why not? They're being held on the flimsiest of legal grounds, and they've got rights."

"Also the right to live. Spring 'em out of jail, even legally, and the Hard Rock'll swarm all over us. Fowler'd find it easy to organize a hanging bee of his own. Moreover, he's made a play for more rope. If we let him have it for a while, mebbe we can tangle him in it. At first I was ready to fight to keep them from taking those men in. Then I saw something in Link that made me realize he hoped we would, which is probably why he mustered so many men to bring along. They could have murdered us. Even Jerome wouldn't have minded, for then he'd be helpin' the law, not violating it himself. Maybe Shadel guessed that, too. Anyway, when I realized he wanted to do the responsible thing, I went along with it. Lands felt the same way."

"I expect you were right," Chance agreed. "Wonder what Fowler's secret game is."

"Well," Ren reflected, "he started under the handicap of a pretty smelly reputation. Meathead's death could be a play for sympathy, and so far he's gained it."

"Which means he wants more power in the association."

"Correct. He can handle Jerome pretty good, already, but there's others he'll have to win around if he's to emerge as a big shot. If he succeeds, the whole Hard Rock better look out." Then, changing the subject, he added, "Been any word from Poison Lake about Indian rustling?"

"Nobody's come in."

"Think I'll ride over there and check before I go back to the roundup."

He ate a hurried late meal at the cookshack, roped a fresh horse from the ranch pasture, and headed on toward Poison Lake. Out there so far from the rest of the embattled Hard Rock, it was hard to realize there was strife and bloodletting anywhere. The spring sun was bright and warm on the land, and here and there early flowers daubed bright splashes on the range, and off to the left the Kettles ran away in a hazy sage-green.

He reached the west line camp shortly after the two punchers stationed there got in from the day's riding. There had been indications of rustling, they reported, although so far they hadn't been able to catch anybody at it.

"Just have to let 'em bleed us awhile," Ren said. "But the roundup'll be here in a few days, and when it's finished everything'll go up into the Kettles."

"Then what?" Johnny Harmon asked.

"We won't run short of worries, but they'll be more concentrated."

He spent the night with the men who, long at their lonely outpost, asked a lot of questions and got a lot of talk out of their own systems. After an early breakfast, he headed east, enroute to the calf roundup that he expected to intercept at the north end of Dry Lake. Two hours' riding brought him in sight of the scarlet minerals of Bloody Rim, gory in a bath of morning sun, and at noon he reached Dry Gap, where he stopped for the noon meal with the men there. Then he headed on for Dry Lake and joined the roundup just as the cocktail guard went on and the day herders came in for their supper.

They had finished the Split Rock branding that day and were holding two herds, one of the ranch's own steers, cows, and calves to be taken to summer range, and a stray cut whose disposition posed a problem.

"Most of the stuff's Joe Garnet's," Ren told Gila, "since we were working next to his range. We'll drive the whole lot over there, and the other outfits can pick up their strays when the so-called official roundup works Joe's range."

Gila gave him a short-tempered frown. "When they're gonna impound ours and shoot any strays found afterward? Looks to me like we ought to hold this bunch for hostages and make 'em go easy on our stuff."

Several other punchers nodded in agreement, and Ren knew he had not overstated the case to Lands when he spoke of their resentment of the abuse their ranch was taking without once striking back in kind.

Patiently, he said, "Look, boys. We're being baited in hopes we'll lose our heads and justify 'em in what they're itchin' to do to us. I'd bet my life that's what Fowler hoped for on the high desert. If we do the right thing with their strays, they'll have far less grounds to hold ours."

"I reckon you're right," Gila said, "but it sure gravels a man."

"It sure does," Ren said wholeheartedly.

Afterward he called Gila aside and told him that Rita might be able to throw light on what had happened at the horse ranch in the case of Meathead.

"He was her watchdog," Gila reflected. "The only man Link'd trust alone with her. I wonder who's ridin' herd on her now?"

"It could be he's decided she don't need to be watched when he's got her boy hidden somewhere to make her behave according to his lights. He might figure that safer, if Meathead gave him trouble, than leaving a man alone with her there."

"I'll see what I can do," Gila agreed, and his eyes showed his eagerness to see the girl again.

"Keep it to yourself," Ren advised, nodding at the other men. "Where you're going and what for. It might not do a bit of good but it's worth a try."

"I'll drift the strays over to Garnet's in the morning," Gila decided, "then take a last sweep along the ridge to see if we missed anything up there. That'll cover my actions. By the way, I seen Garnet this morning. He said there was another session of the association last night. Their roundup's startin' next week way down south on Cat Track. It's gonna keep everybody else busy, and they figure Link's got a stake in the ruckus now, even if he ain't a cowman."

"So?"

"So they appointed him to police our outlaw roundup while they're down in the other end of the country."

"I thought so," Ren exclaimed. "It's what he was after."

"And we can count on some heavy-handed policing from him."

"What does Garnet think about it?"

"I had a feelin' Joe don't like belonging to that association and would pull out of it now if he dared."

CHAPTER NINE

Gila trailed out with a cut of nearly seventy strays, breachy stock that since the fall before had drifted in from neighboring ranges, Crown, Big N, 7X, and Joe Garnet's JG. The morning was fair and warm, and the puncher called to Ren, for the sake of the others nearby, "Mebbe I'll come back along the ridge to see if we missed anything," and Ren nodded. The outfit would work Bloody Rim that day, back under Ren's supervision, and Gila would rejoin it there if he didn't get himself in a jam with Fowler's hard cases. He hazed the cattle northeast, heading for Marsh Creek and the low crowns of the Turkey Hills, which barely showed on the light-streaked horizon.

The cattle he drove had been bunched long enough to hold together without much trouble, and two hours later he reached the Marsh Creek sink. Afterward he followed the stream until he was well inside Garnet's boundary, and there he turned the cattle loose. He debated a moment between heading at once for Turkey Neck and the horse outfit on Deacon Creek, but he had a strong wish to make sure Garnet, and especially Libby, realized how fairly Ren had handled their strays. Accepting an extra ride of several miles, he headed for their headquarters at the edge of the hills.

It didn't disappoint him to find, when he came in among the cottonwoods sheltering the buildings, that Garnet was off somewhere. He rode clear up to the picket fence surrounding the house before he saw Libby, down on her hands and knees on the other side, weeding a flower bed. He had arrived quietly, and when she looked up and saw him watching her, she was startled and a little angry and wholly unaware of a smudge of dirt at one side of her nose.

"Don't you know enough to let a person know you're coming, Gila Veyan?" she demanded. "Especially at a time like this."

He laughed. "You ain't that scared of Two C, Libby. But you sure seem scared of somebody. Could it be somebody on your own side of this squabble?"

She smiled reluctantly. "What're you doing in enemy country?"

There had always been an easy way between them that did not exist between her and Ren, and he knew she trusted him. She was an appealing girl he would have been gone on long ago had he not already lost his heart to Rita.

"Wanted to tell you I threw back some association strays. Left 'em down the crick on your grass. Some're your dad's, and the other association outfits can pick up theirs when they brand here."

Her mouth opened. "Other outfits? You mean you aren't holding *any* association strays?"

"Due strictly to what you deny in Ren Tyler. Common sense. Libby, you know he can't be as bad as you've tried to think, and don't tell me you don't realize he'd die for you in a minute."

Stiffly, she said, "That doesn't put him on the right side."

Gila pointed a finger at her. "Nobody's gonna make me believe he ain't the man who, not very long ago, you figured to make permanent in your life, and you're lettin' him down and so's your dad."

"Why," she gasped. "How can you say that?"

"Because Ren and Chance and us Two C boys're fightin' what's also your fight."

"So we want sheep in the basin?" she said incredulously.

"Them sheep's got precious little to do with what's going on. Link Fowler's got somethin' up his sleeve, and Joe Garnet must've mentioned it to you in his worry. None of us knows what, just yet, but if your dad had the sense God gave to geese, he'd throw in on the side he can trust and not with men who might gobble him up in the shambles that's coming." Gila shook the finger. "As for you—well, if you were half a woman you wouldn't throw away your happiness and Ren's because you don't happen to agree with him."

"Well—well—!" Libby pulled in a deep breath. Then, stamping her foot, "Isn't the issue confused enough without you bringing up things like that? Get out of here!"

Grinning, he said, "Tell Joe what I said, and think it over yourself. It gets plainer every day Link Fowler's runnin' his own private coon, and that coon just could be the little outfits around him, like yours and Varley Eden's, which would sure go under if Two C does." He touched his hat to her and rode on.

At noon he was on Deacon Creek and still in the juniper, and he stopped to loosen the cinch and remove the bridle bit so his horse could graze. He ate a couple of cold biscuits he had carried in a saddle pocket and then took a drink at the creek and leisurely smoked a cigarette. The serenity of his surroundings seeped into him, and he savored the tobacco and warm slope breeze and the grandeur of the country about him. Then he considered the ticklish job ahead of him.

He wanted to get on the cuesta formation from which he had checked Fowler's place the last time he slipped in to see Rita, but to reach it he had to cross considerable open country, a riskier business by daylight. When his horse began to show disinterest in the bunch grass around it, he readied it for riding, let it drink, and rose to the saddle. He struck down the grade, aiming himself at an angle that carried him north of the horse ranch. When he broke onto the basin floor, he dropped immediately into a dry wash he remembered from the days when he had ridden for Fowler.

He moved due east for better than an hour, not hurrying because the loose sand tired the horse. Finally he dismounted and walked up the bank to the top, where he took an intent look at the country wheeling before him, seeing no one. He went back and led up the horse, then rode due south. If he were surprised by one of the mustangers, it was unlikely that Rita would be compromised by it. Fowler had no reason as yet to suspect a continuing friendship between her and Wad's old saddlemate.

Another half hour brought him to the rear of the cuesta that had been his objective. He left the horse at the foot of the slope and went on afoot and then, keeping carefully hidden, gradually worked his way to a good viewpoint on the rim above the ranch buildings and trees. By then the racket had told him that the wild-horse breaking was still going on here, and now he could see the dust hanging over the traps and keeping him from a good look at them.

He lay flat on the hot, rocky surface, unsure whether the whole outfit was at the corrals, but seeing no one elsewhere around the sprawling and cluttered yard. The shabby house also appeared deserted, but there was little doubt that Rita was in there, keeping to herself. She would emerge for wood, water, or for some other purpose eventually. When she did, he hoped to attract her attention with the little mirror he carried in his shirt pocket. Then he would wait until she could slip out to him, even if that meant deep in the coming night.

The unshaded earth on which he lay began to bake him with its absorbed heat, and now and then he pulled out a bandanna to mop his face. The work at the traps went on steadily, and he began to despair of Rita's showing herself where he could see her. Twice men came into the yard below him from the direction of the corrals and went to the well to drink, and each time he pulled back and lay uneasily waiting until it was safe to show his head again at the chewed, rocky edge of the drop. Then, somewhere between five and six, they all knocked off and came up to wash for supper. He got his first head count then and accounted not only for Fowler and Roddy, but the others who made up the outfit. They went immediately into the house to eat, and, so quickly it seemed she was trying to stay away from them as far as possible, Rita appeared on the porch.

She looked tired, hot, and bedraggled and for a moment leaned against a roof post, pushing her hair back from her forehead with a restless hand. He had pulled the mirror from his pocket, checked the position of the sun, and as her eyes swept across the yard the light struck them, and he saw her body tense. He hoped earnestly that no one inside was watching her, but she recovered instantly, her gaze running to the rim top and catching the friendly wave of his hand. She knew he was no enemy, and there could be only one friend who would dare this—himself. He slid the mirror back into his pocket, waiting for her to react and give him some sign of where they could meet.

But she turned and hurried back indoors, and he hoped that it was only because somebody had yelled for her to come and wait on the table. His resentment of her being a menial in this tawdry household ran through him caustically, and he ached for a way to take her out of it this very night without jeopardizing her prospect of eventually recovering her child. At least he was working on it. If she could help him incriminate Fowler for the murder of Meathead, it could well be the way to her freedom. To him that meant even more than justice for the sheepherders confined in the Alkali jail.

In about twenty minutes, the men came out of the house in close succession, Fowler and Roddy bringing up the rear. The latter two went back to the corrals, while the others strolled idly across to the bunkhouse, rolling and lighting smokes. They went indoors, and he hoped it was to start one of the evening card games that were the mainstay of bunk-house pastimes. Glancing the other way, he saw Fowler and his foreman at the horse corrals. They were roping and sad-dling mounts. He lay with baited breath until they rose to saddle and rode out, fearing they would move in the direction that would show them his horse. He let out a sigh when they headed south, and he decided they were paying an evening visit to Crown.

It was another ten minutes before Rita came onto the porch again, although she didn't even glance his way. She strolled leisurely across the yard toward the creek and became nearly lost in the trees, but he could see that she had stopped there with her back to the trunk of a cottonwood, somberly regarding the water. Again she waited, and he watched the bunkhouse for somebody to check on her action, in the event one of them had been delegated to replace the dead giant as her guardian.

No one showed any interest, and this was what she was waiting to determine, too, for she turned then and began to walk slowly up the creek. Gila's mouth formed a soft smile at her stratagem. He would meet her far enough up the creek, they would know if anyone followed her later, and he could cut out of sight. Then she would pretend to be up to nothing more than getting some of the cooler night air.

Withdrawing from his position, Gila rose and slipped down to his waiting horse. The cuesta cut him from view of the bunkhouse, letting him cross the open ground and ride directly into the creek timber about a quarter mile above the house. Rita was waiting there for him. Her mouth formed a grave smile when he stepped down from the horse, but she said nothing.

"It's all right," he assured her. "Nobody so much as stuck

his head out to keep tabs on you. I take it Link and Roddy went up to Crown."

She shook her head. "He was talking about meeting somebody about something. He told the men to keep themselves handy till he comes back. I don't know what's up, but they're excited."

"Then I've got to hurry. Rita, what really happened to Meathead? I take it you know he was killed and that they're blamin' Two C for it and managed to get two of our men locked up."

Her face hardened. "I know. I heard them talking. And your men aren't guilty. Link Fowler killed him, and it was my fault."

"So Meathead bothered you."

"Never," she cried. "But I said he had. I didn't expect to get him killed. I only hoped they'd quit leaving Meathead here alone with me, or any other man. Then maybe I could get away. Maybe I could find my baby. He must be in California, one of the towns where they deliver horses. Link Fowler hasn't been anyplace else in years. But I know I couldn't find him, and that was just foolish hope."

"So far," Gila agreed. "But we can break his hold on you if we can get a stronger one on him."

"I don't want to help hang him, Gila. In spite of everything."

"I know, and I won't use anything you tell me except to help get your baby back."

Softly, she said, "You liked Wad a lot, didn't you?"

"We were side-kicks." He caught her hands. "But it's mostly you, Rita. I reckon I fell in love with you as soon as he did, but he had the inside track."

Incredulity stamped her face, and her eyes filled with tears. "You, Gila? Then it isn't right to let you risk your life for me. Everything I had like that died with him."

"I'm not askin' a thing."

"No," she mused, "you wouldn't. I'll tell you anything I can."

"You said Link killed the kid because you accused him of bothering you. Is that the only reason you think so?"

"Well, it was queer his saying he spent all that day in the breaks. He hardly goes anywhere alone and usually takes Roddy. Yet not that one day, and maybe I know why. Roddy wouldn't stop at a killing, but he really liked Meathead. There'd be trouble right now if he thought the way I do."

"They think it was the sheepherders. Ren Tyler says they were really out for blood when they come to the camp."

She nodded. "And that's all I know about that. But I heard something at suppertime about this thing tonight. Link said the kettle had to boil over before they could get anywhere, and this time they'd see it did. That mean anything?"

"Mebbeso. Ren says they're tryin' to bait us into some hotheaded move of our own to prove we're the outlaw outfit they've branded us. So far he's kept from it and tended strictly to business, so much so Two C's apt to stand up under what they've done with their deadline, outlawing and blacklisting. That don't suit the association, which seems to boil down, actually, to Link Fowler and Pearce Jerome. They want us destroyed, Jerome for spite and Fowler—I'd say for gain."

"So the pot boils over—" Rita began.

"Yeah. When they get us so hoppin' mad we go wild, they'll be justified in a real range war. And their chances are good. Our boys and Lands' men are about ready to let fly, right now." Gila wrinkled his brow. "I'll see you again real soon, now that they give you a little leeway. Every evening after supper you take this little walk so they'll get used to it. Sometimes I'll be here, and if you don't show I'll know you don't dare. Link and Roddy rode south, and if they're meetin' somebody, I bet it's a party from Crown again. I'm going to ride up that way."

"Oh—be careful."

He squeezed her hand, mounted, and rode upstream into the thickening dusk.

The night steadily deepened, the familiar landmarks of the day dissolving in vague patterns of mystery, and as he rode he drew the last cold biscuit from a saddle pocket and consumed it leisurely. Presently he angled over until he cut the east basin's lengthwise road, but he only skirted it, hoping thus to catch sight of Fowler without being seen. For the same reason he denied himself the smoke he wanted after he had finished the biscuit.

He had ridden nearly half an hour when a party of approaching riders drummed a warning on the road. He reined in, staring forward through the night's first starshine. In a moment they took shape, and a scowl pressed onto his face. There were around a dozen of them, riding fast toward Fowler's horse ranch and too far away to be identified. He sat quietly, letting them pass on to the north, then swung his horse back along his own off-trail course, hurrying to keep apace with them. Something big was up, sure enough, and he wanted to know more about it.

He was sure Fowler's headquarters were the party's immediate destination well before it turned in on the lane. He reined up again while the night riders receded swiftly up the lane and became lost in the trees below the cuesta. True to his prediction, they were not long in returning, augmented by the men who had waited in Fowler's bunkhouse. When they struck the main road they turned north in a body, and, his throat tightening, he divined their destination.

The high desert again. Whatever the secret purposes in Fowler's head, his men and the Crown bunch with them had been thoroughly incensed by the killing, according to Ren's account, and had wanted a lot more than the arrest of the herders. But Ren and Lands had seen through it and did not resist the arrests, and the sheriff had managed to work

Pearce Jerome into a spot where he dared not defy the law. So these men would not be hard to lead into a reprisal attack in which Two C would have to make an outright fight, loosening the full fury of warfare.

He waited until they were lost in the distance, then cut a beeline for Turkey Neck and the roundup camp.

CHAPTER TEN

The cattle work at Dry Gap was within a day of completion, and while he ate supper in the early evening, Ren watched the herd, out across the flat, that he would send to the Kettles the next day while moving the roundup west to Poison Lake. His punchers sat around with their suppers in their laps, and off in the twilight the nighthawk was hazing the *remuda* out to its night's grass. The cocktail guard slowly circled the herd, the cook fire was dying in its pit, and the camp had the lazy air a cowhand found so comforting at the end of a hard day's toil.

Gila had been gone since morning, but Ren wasn't worried about him as yet for it had been probable that he would have to wait until night to make contact with Rita, if he managed to do so at all. But the men didn't understand the real reason for his absence, and they were beginning to wonder about him. So Ren wasn't surprised when Flint Hollister dropped his empty plate and cup in the wreck pan by the wagon and walked over to him.

"How about me taking a ride up to the ridge?" he said. "With the hassle that's going on, Gila could've had trouble."

"He'll be back all right," Ren said.

"What makes you so confident?"

"We both knew he might be out late." The listening men looked puzzled, so he added, "We figured it worth a little time to spy on Fowler's headquarters and see what they really do with themselves."

That satisfied them, and Hollister pulled out his jackknife and began to play mumblety-peg. When Jim Fanning was through with his meal, he and Joe Parsons started to match coins, while old Abe Jewett spread his bed under the wagon and stretched out on it. The rest, equally tired, followed his example.

Ren walked to the fire and refilled his cup with coffee, then, his back propped to his bedroll, shaped up a cigarette and lighted it. Now and then his eyes strayed toward distant Marsh Creek, and he wondered how Joe Garnet had taken his unexpected return of the association strays, when he had had every right to retain them. He had been tempted to take them over himself, but at the last moment had changed his mind, for he didn't like to be reminded of Libby's stubborn hostility toward him.

He was on the point of turning in too, when, far away, a swiftly ridden horse drummed its announcement through the night. The camp came alive again, half-dressed men standing erect to scan the darkness to the east of them. Then the rushing horse slowed down, indicating that its rider knew a herd was being held here.

"Gila, at last," somebody muttered. "From the way he was larrapun' it, he sure must be hungry."

In a few minutes Gila rode in, and one look at him told Ren that something was seriously wrong. He waited in a sudden mounting of tension.

Gila was breathing heavily from his hard riding and said huskily, "Boys, hit leather! A good part of the east basin's barrelin' toward the sheep, right now! Fowler's leadin' 'em, and this time it's probably a butcherin' party—!"

Ren needed to know no more, for Gila wasn't a man who rattled. He snapped, "Get ready to ride, boys. Guns and plenty of shells."

"We're gonna give it back to 'em finally?" somebody yelled.

"You heard me."

That changed the stunned confusion to swift action, and men slid into their clothes, armed themselves, and went legging it for the night horses. Two C had been temperate beyond bearing, but now it would hit back. By the time Ren led his own mount back to the fire, Gila was gulping down a cup of coffee.

"You stay, Abe," Ren said to the near-by cook, who had buckled his gun on. "But ride out and tell the boys on night herd they won't be relieved for a spell."

A moment afterward he was riding north with ten men, hardly three quarters the number Gila estimated to be with Fowler. They were also two hours behind, but had less ground to cover to reach the high desert. So it was just possible that they could make it in time to head off the attack on the flocks.

Somebody had brought Gila a fresh horse, and, tired as he was, he kept pace with Ren. "Seen Rita," he yelled above the racket of their traveling. "Give you the details later, but we're right about Fowler killing the kid. She also said Link aims to boil the kettle over, tonight. She's gonna help us, and I've arranged so I can see her again."

"Good," Ren answered.

He knew he had a tough nut to crack, for the night's advantages were all on Fowler's side. The three sheep bands were scattered two or three miles apart, and the attackers could feint at one and strike at another, or they could split and attack two or all of them at once. No matter what use was made of the Two C men, Fowler could change tactics and get around them, while there was every chance that they would arrive too late to do any good at all.

They splashed over Marsh Creek and soon thereafter struck the climb to the peneplain that gave rise to the high desert.

The terrain was perilous for a fast-moving horse at best, and in the night the hazard was multiplied. But the only slowing they did was out of consideration for the horses, and presently the belt of gully washes and rock scabs was behind them. The high starshine gave them fair vision, and when they came onto the smoother slope they could again pick up speed. At the end of about forty minutes, Ren lifted an arm in warning, then slowed, and stopped his horse.

No order to keep quiet was needed. Every ear keened the darkness for alien impact, the sound of massed travel, or the sound of shooting. Only the desert's murmuring silence came to them, and they rode on, topping the ridge ahead and seeing below them the dying fire of a sheep camp. Beyond that was the dark mass of the first sheep band.

Yancy Lands was at the wagon with the two men he had used to replace the jailed Corbett and Botwood. All three stood with rifles in their hands and well out of the firelight, although the approach to the camp had been open.

"What now?" Lands said, when Ren rode up to him.

"War party coming, mebbe twenty men. We damned near killed some good horses to get here to help. And I'm gonna ask you to damn' near kill your sheep."

Lands gawked at him. "Kill 'em? How?"

"By keeping 'em moving so fast and so long Fowler's wolf pack can't connect with 'em. They figure on surprise, and our only chance to upset 'em is for you not to be where they think you are."

Lands nodded reluctantly. "Hate to beat up the critters, but you're right."

"Get at it. Leave the wagons where they are and the fires going. We want to fool 'em as long as we can. The boys and me'll try to see they don't get close to anything that can't shoot back."

Lands barked orders at the two listening herders, who sprang into motion, whistling to their dogs. Under their control, Ren knew by now, the flocks could be moved with the darting cohesion of mercury drops. But the animals always blatted when on the move, which made it essential to get them beyond earshot of their present feeding grounds.

Swinging to look at Gila, he said, "Divide the boys among the three sheep wagons. Be sure they fort so they won't get hit if Fowler aims to sneak in and shoot up a camp. Tell 'em to lay low till they're sure what they face. If it's a split party, they can cut loose and try to break it up. If the party's still together, try to get a man off to the rest of us so we can unite, too. Meanwhile, I'm gonna see if I can slow Fowler enough for the sheep to get out of hearing."

He had no time to lose and wheeled away from them, striking due east. Fowler's party had had to follow the east basin road to skirt the Turkey Hills, and it would keep to the road for easier night traveling and then head west to the sheep range. It would pick the easiest going in the open country, also, which let him judge where to connect with them, as he must.

After fifteen minutes he could no longer hear the sheep himself, but he went on for another mile or so before deciding to make his play. He was following down a shallow draw falling from the high desert, which he expected them to use, and he angled away from it on its south slope for another short distance. Dismounting, he dragged and threw together a pile of dead desert brush, struck a match, and set it burning. He piled more brush on the mounting blaze, then, satisfied, took his tally book and a stubby pencil from his pocket.

Tearing a tag of paper from the book, he wrote, "Fowler, they're laying for you. Be careful. A friend." He stuck the dead stick in the ground, impaled the message on it, plainly visible in the growing light, then mounted, and rode on to the crest.

He left his horse on the blind side and slipped back afoot to wait and watch. The fire would attract their attention, even if they were a mile or so off the course he had reckoned. They were less than human if they did not investigate, giving Lands more time to get the sheep away, and the warning ought to make them too uneasy to split into parties and launch separate attacks.

He had barely set it up in time, for in less than five minutes the earth carried the sound of heavy travel, and, scanning the belowground, he detected them, slowing as they started up the climb. Almost at once they stopped and huddled, and, while he could see nothing but obscure smears in the night, he knew their attention had been caught by the mysterious fire on the empty desert. He lay tensely, waiting while they came on up the draw, then they angled off warily toward the burning brush, keeping prudently together.

He watched them halt and study the strange situation ahead before they rode into it, then they came on slowly. In a moment, as they grew plainer, he began to frown. Gila had estimated them at around twenty men, but he pegged this bunch at no more than a dozen. Either Gila had been wrong in his hasty appraisal, or they had already split in two. These were Fowler's mustangers with a handful of punchers from Crown, and Jerome was not present. Either the old fire-eater had chosen to keep out of it, or was leading the other party. He didn't see Hunk Roddy, either, and Roddy wouldn't miss a thing like this if he could help it.

Fowler rode into the distinct light of the flames and reached down to snatch the paper from its fastening. Ren knew he had read it when he pushed back his hat and handed the message to one of the Crown men. There was no guessing what was said, but the matter touched off an argument. Fowler won and led the party on up the draw toward the sheep range.

Ren dogged them at a cautious distance, and, where the draw shallowed on a low backbone, stopped his horse in the realization that his ruse had worked as far as it went. Whatever their original intentions, this party had become sufficiently worried to stay together, whereas it might have split to put a third party in the field against the three flocks. They rode slowly, quietly, bearing down on the nearest camp, whose dying fire glowed like a cigar tip in the distance below them.

His hope of averting the attack had become one of minimizing the damage, which meant stalling for more time. Fowler had had to put down an argument against defying the warning, and it might help to make the others regret that defiance. Pulling his six-gun, Ren emptied it, scattering them into cover like scared rabbits and also warning the men at the camp.

CHAPTER ELEVEN

Fowler, on his previous visits to the sheep camp, seemed to have paid particular attention to the physical setting, with something of this nature in mind. He had brought his bristling force along a shallow wash dropping from the ridge, which would have let him spread it on a line that commanded the camp. But the shots had caught his party while mounted and still short of its objective, impacting on nerves already disturbed by the mysterious fire and warning.

Now the mustangers' exhortations punctuated the crash of horses and riders through the desert brush, split between frantic orders and angry cursing. Ren had not hoped to rout them, but Fowler feared that result and demanded that his men secure their mounts and advance on the camp on foot. They seemed to be obeying him, for presently the racket stopped. They had at least taken cover to wait for the situation to clarify.

Ren muddled it again, shouting as if to men of his own, "Some of you boys get in on their left! We'll handle this side! Stay where you are, at the camp! We'll drive the sons your way!"

He knew the deception would not mislead his own men, who realized how thinly Two C had had to spread itself tonight. He dismounted, tied his horse, and made a ducked-over run. From a new position, a moment later, he finished emptying his pistol.

Red streaks cut the night below him, and while he thumbed in fresh cartridges the rattle of gunfire battered his ears. They were blazing away in all directions, he discerned, including the empty position he had just put behind. Caught now in the forewarned trap, none of them would be very bold until they discovered that much of it was sham. He moved farther left and whammed in more shots, a reckless energy singing in him. If he could teach this ugly lot a thumping lesson, it would shatter Fowler's growing hold on the stockmen's association. He knew there was only an outside chance of his doing it. He had had to cover three scattered sheep camps with a dozen fighting men. Little more than half the men Gila had judged to be with Fowler earlier were with him here. Roddy or Jerome or both could be leading smaller forces against the other camps.

He saw that his men had grasped his purpose and were adding to it. At least two of them had got on the slant across the draw from Fowler and were pinging bullets off the scab rock in which the raiders had tried to hide. From the camp two more were firing at an oblique angle. They were using his tactic of moving between shots. This made Fowler's force, pumping lead recklessly, waste most of it harmlessly in the voids.

Determined to keep them unbalanced, Ren crept back to his horse, halting there only long enough to get his bearings. Fire stabs punctured the night below him while he watched, with his ears jarred by disturbed air. The night riders, he could now see, had filtered into a shallow rock crop in their frenzy to fort where they could protect themselves on all sides. Now and then somebody threw a random shot up the slope toward him. The scab was not deep enough to protect the horses, so they must be cut off from him by the sage-clad slope on the west.

He untied his horse and, leading it, started to circle carefully around. He drew no fire. They had begun to guess that there were fewer guns against them than they had thought. He worked downslope again, drawing west of Fowler's position. Then he saw their horses, farther out on his right. Someone had been detailed to take them there, after the raiders had dismounted, and must have gone back to the fight. When he had angled closer to them, he still could see no guard. He turned the matter over in his mind, then mounted, and rode down to where they waited, uneasily stirring and tossing their heads.

The dozen animals were tied to the low clumps of sage and dead rabbit brush. Swinging down, he began to loosen the reins and throw them back over the horses' heads. He moved slowly, quietly, doing nothing to agitate them until the last was free. Then he whacked one with his hat and let out a yell. The hit horse went bolting away, towing the others, those with shoes striking sparks from the rocks.

From the scab rock came a sharp, protesting outcry. Ren swung to fling a shot that way, then went up to saddle. Three or four men came racing his way, not fully grasping the situation, but aware of the escaping *remuda*. He drove them back, then rode a shallow semicircle that brought him in on the far side of the sheep camp. He left his horse where his riders had secured theirs, then darted in to where Frank Landusky and Jim Fanning were holding that side of the skirmish line.

When he crawled up to Fanning, the latter muttered, "You sure tangled Link's rope. Only, how're we gonna handle so many, now they know they're cornered and have got to fight it out?"

"We don't fight it out," Ren said. "They can't do any damage here, and they're harmless without horses. Who's across the wash from 'em?"

"Pete and Flint."

"As soon as I can tell 'em, we're lighting out. I'm pretty

convinced there's another party or two up here. And they could still raise hell."

He crossed the draw, circled in to Hollister and Farraday, and told them to pull out as quietly as possible and rejoin the men at the sheep wagon. He stayed there a while after they had left, shooting from one position and then another, hoping to let Fowler waste some more ammunition. On his own way back to the camp, he detoured to pick up the picketed draft horses used to move the sheep wagon. A few moments later, his party of five was mounted.

Ren led the old draft plugs far enough away to be of no use to Fowler, then halted the party for a moment to take a look at the rear. The baffled raiders were still blazing away, but the shooting was tapering off.

"I'd give a pretty," Landusky commented, "for a picture of Link's face when he finds out what happened to him."

"If there's a second bunch," Fanning said, "which camp would they be apt to hit, Ren?"

"The one to the east would be the closest for them. We'll check that first."

Free to travel, they did so at a reckless speed. Lands had called the camp they put behind his No. 1, and No. 2 was farther east and north, on the slope of the high desert. No. 3 was well to the west, but it could have been chosen for the very reason that its remoteness made it seem an illogical target. There was a further chance that the second raiding party had divided for a nuisance attack on both camps. They whipped over the ridge and kept going pell-mell, slanting down the slow fall of the land.

Twenty minutes later, Ren knew he had made a bad guess. Lands had got the sheep removed from Camp No. 2, also, and when the riders raised the sheep wagon and pulled down, nothing but the night's murmuring silence came to them. Either there was no second raiding party, or it had gone in force to hit the camp over west. They went on toward the wagon.

Their open manner told the men there who they were. One of those waiting was Lands, and the other three were Two C punchers. They had waited in the fireless camp for the past hour without any cause for alarm.

"Well, I could be wrong," Ren admitted. "But Hunk Roddy wasn't with Fowler, and he's not a man to stay out of a scrap. Furthermore, Fowler had only a little more than half the men Gila counted leaving the horse ranch, and Gila knows how to count. I think there's another bunch that stuck together and, if they've made a hit, it was on the west camp."

"Or," Lands said darkly, "they're lookin' for one of the flocks."

Ren had considered that and dismissed it. He shook his head. "That bunch wants a shootin' war with Two C, itself. At least we'd better check that camp before we look anywhere else. Gila there?"

"Yeah," Lands said. "If Roddy's over there with the rest of their men, you'll need me and the boys."

Ren agreed. He had gained an advantage over Fowler by rattling him at the very start and exploiting that to the limit. But by now the possible other party could have hit something, somewhere, and dug in. If it were the west camp, Gila and the three men with him would need all the help they could get.

Lands had only recently come over from the west camp, in his rounds to scatter the sheep bands, and Ren let him take the lead. The footing in that area was treacherous, so they rode in file, no longer able to get the utmost from their tiring mounts. They crested the land swell and started down the west slope, the strike of bunched hoofs the only sound in the night. They had to come to the bottom of this slant and mount a higher one to the west to reach the next camp.

Starlight lay thinly on the irregular distance, and the night wind shook a soft murmur out of the desert brush. They came to the bottom, where the cut banks of an empty wash broke their speed. The horses pitched down, and when the last of them had crossed and climbed out, Lands spoke in clipped suddenness.

"Listen!"

Only then did Ren hear it above the stir of air on the foliage, a faraway and softened sound. It was like the dripping of water, but less regular in rhythm.

"That's them," Lands said gustily. "Ren, I sure hope you've got a knot to tie in their tails, too."

"Not a chance," Ren grunted. "Come on."

They had reached a vast open slope that made good sheep pasture until the hot winds of summer seared it and wiped out the water supply. Up at its top was Two Fingers, a landmark of pinnacles rising from a common rock base. Ren knew Lands had established this camp on its leeward side, and it was at present cut off from them by the rocks. That gave them a chance to move up quietly, gaining what they could from surprise. But the downslopes all around the pinnacles would offset that, for they would have to fight their way upgrade.

They rode swiftly to the blind side of Two Fingers and dismounted. The water drip had changed to an intensity of sound that percussed their ears. Lands was the only one of them who had seen this camp, and he described it briefly.

"Wagon's close to the rocks. Springs come out there. Our boys'd fort up there. So it's likely Roddy's anchored his ends at the base of the rock and drew a horseshoe around 'em. That way he could take his time."

Ren nodded. "We'd better split and come in along the rock from both sides. We can't hit their rear without danger to our own men."

"We'll have to bust loose their anchors," Lands agreed, "and throw 'em back to where we can get at 'em."

They divided the men, and Ren took his half to the right, while the flockmaster slipped off in the other direction. It would be ticklish, until they cleared the edge of the rocks and no longer risked shooting into each other's positions. He led his squad along the rough bajada under the rock, slowly rounding westward, the sound of the forward shooting sharpening. Then he halted, motioned for the others to wait, and went on alone until he could see the crosshatch of fire streaks in the boulder-dotted foreground. Two of Gila's men were on this side of the sheep wagon. Lands had been right about Roddy's throwing his men into a horseshoe whose ends touched the base of the vaulting rock and formed a trap.

Moving back until his men could see him, he motioned them forward. Whispering, when they came up to him, he said, "We've gotta pick off the two men the farthest this way. Frank and me'll slip in as close as we can before they catch on. Then you others move up, and we'll try to join up with our boys."

Landusky stepped forward, and the two of them began to inch their way through the shadowed rocks under the big monolith. A moment later Ren had spotted the man he meant to tackle, who lay behind a fabricated breastwork about twenty feet out. He crept forward, knowing he could be dropped by one of his own men if they spotted him. But it was somebody farther out on Roddy's line who did so, and a voice cut through the racket.

"Arizona—look out—behind you!"

The man ahead rolled over and sat up. Ren yelled at him to freeze, while every man in Roddy's party seemed to start shooting his way. He flung himself into cover, waited a second, then started to crawl. The man he had stalked had moved off into the rocks somewhere.

He yelled, "Gila! It's me, Ren! We're comin' in!"

A tired voice that was not Gila's answered, "Come ahead!"

Hunk Roddy's voice bucketed against the rocks. "Stop 'em, boys! Keep 'em separated!"

Ren kept crawling forward, and behind him came Fanning, Hollister, and Farraday. Roddy's men were already drawing back, the dwindling shooting making Lands' voice audible as he moved his men in. The flockmaster seemed to be making a juncture with the other side of the sheep camp. The night riders called back and forth, too, but Ren made out nothing that was said. Roddy seemed to be reforming them, undiscouraged, for of a sudden a straightened line, bristling with flashing gunfire, and a barrage of bullets rained across the camp and adjoining rocks.

Ren had emptied and reloaded his hot pistol three times before the fury of it abated. When it did so, it was all at once. The downslope shooting halved, then halved again, and he realized they were fighting a rear-guard action while they tried to pull out. He was willing to settle for that, but he called for a charge. They would be less apt to leave here and hunt up another target if he could turn it into a rout.

His men slid through the rocks with him, peppering the heels of the retreating invaders. When the cover thinned out, Roddy's dispirited outfit had to go bolting for the horses, which were now in view down the slope. Then Ren realized why Roddy had put up a stiff action to cover his retreat. Down there a man was carrying another over his shoulder. Closer this way, two more were helping a third, practically dragging him along with them.

"Hold it!" he shouted to his men. "They've got some wounded they're tryin' to get away."

The silence that had come down on the scene seemed to make its own impact on his ears. Down there in the obscurity, men were mounting and riding off, not waiting for the rest. Two of them were lashing a limp figure to one of the saddles. Then they swung up, and one of them led the horse away. Abruptly, there was only empty space down there.

Turning away, Ren walked up to the sheep wagon. The sternness of his face deepened when he saw some of his men hunkered over something on the ground. He hurried forward, and by the time he got there, a lantern had been lighted. His throat constricted. The man on the ground was Gila Veyan.

"How bad?" he asked.

Watson glanced up. "He's alive, but that's about all. Got it in the openin' round, and we couldn't do a thing to help him. Had all we could manage standin' them bastards off."

Ren dropped to his knees while somebody spilled lantern light over Gila's still shape. His whole shirt front was soaked with blood, and he didn't seem to breathe. But there was a pulse, thin, thready, rapid. Ren fought back the emotion that tore along his nerves, then words punched out.

"Couple of you go for the doctor, and be careful you don't run into that bunch. Come back by Joe Garnet's. That's the closest ranch. If Gila can be moved, we'll have him down there by the time you get back. If we're not there, we'll be here."

Two of them wheeled away; he didn't take time to see who. Somebody had already built a fire to heat water. Another had entered the sheep wagon and come out with a herder's white shirt, soap, and a bottle of disinfectant. Ren slit open Gila's V-necked shirt, exposing his bloody chest. But the wound had stopped bleeding, an ugly hole midway between the navel and right ribs. It had missed the lungs and maybe the liver, but a gut wound could be as mean as either.

"Movin' won't do him any good," Lands was saying in Ren's ear.

"No, but what chance would he have here? Know how to make a horse litter?"

"Ought to." Lands moved away.

When the water was heated, Ren cleansed, disinfected,

and bound Gila's wound. It left the patient no better and no worse. By then Lands had the litter ready. As gently as possible, Gila was started on the long journey down to Joe Garnet's ranch. Only Lands remained behind, for he wanted to check on his scattered flocks.

CHAPTER TWELVE

Camp No. 1 gave no sign that fury had spent itself there, too, in recent hours. Ren had left his solemn, slow-moving men and come on to find that Link Fowler and his men had left, perforce on foot. Under other circumstances, the grim-faced ramrod would have chuckled at the picture they must have made, high-heeled and hapless and many miles from home. What he would feel toward Fowler from that night on was a far cry from amusement.

He rode directly overland, thereafter, following the beeline course he and his men had taken coming out. He had lost track of time, but before long grew aware of the morning star and realized that a new day was about born. He dropped down through the roughs on the edge of the high desert, and in the half-light of dawn rode into Garnet's Marsh Creek headquarters.

His hail had brought Joe to the back porch. Chimney smoke showed that a breakfast fire was burning, which meant that Libby might be up and just beyond the open door. The rancher stood stiffly, silently, reminding Ren that on their last encounter Joe had informed him he was no longer welcome. He pulled up at the edge of the porch and looked with weary eyes at the rancher.

"If you don't mind," he said, "the boys are fetchin' a hurt man here. He might even be dead by that time. Gila Veyan."

"Gila?" Garnet stared. "What happened to him?"

"Shot in the belly, last night. On the high desert. Your *amigos* paid a visit up there and got more than they bargained for. But Gila was hit."

He saw Libby in the doorway then, stiff and pale.

"Don't like to move him any farther than needed," he resumed. "If it's all right to bring him here."

"Of course it is," Libby said tightly. Her father nodded his head. Then she faltered, "Ren, who did it?"

"Fowler and Hunk Roddy run the show."

The look she flung her father could have singed his hair.

Ren told them what had happened, which, had Gila been spared, would have ended in a one-sided fiasco for the ambitious mustanger and the jealous old cowman on Crown. Its effect was less than he had hoped. Both were clearly shocked by the development, but they seemed no less stiff and detached with him. He was too tired to worry about it now.

Libby said, "I'll get a bed ready," and turned back into the house. Joe motioned for Ren to swing down, then wordlessly led the horse toward the barn. Ren crossed the porch and helped himself to a drink from the water bucket, then sat down on the wash bench and rolled a cigarette.

He had finished smoking by the time Joe came back. The rancher said, "Breakfast'll be ready soon as Libby's through makin' the bed. You better wash-up."

It was an offer of hospitality, and Ren decided to accept it. He got wearily to his feet and scrubbed up, then combed his hair. Joe had gone into the house, and he knew Libby had come into the kitchen, for he could hear things rattling in there. When he walked to the door, he saw her at the stove. Her father had gone on into another room. He stepped in just as she turned with a plate of biscuits in her hands. Her eyes met his.

"I know Gila's more than another rider to you," she said. "I'm sorry about him, Ren."

He nodded, and she motioned him to a chair and called

her father. He had no hunger, which wasn't conspicuous, for neither of them did, either. Their minds were on the procession coming off the high desert, as his was. All were thinking that a man shot through the belly hadn't much chance of life.

Gila was still alive when the men came in with him a little before eight o'clock. They carried him to the extra bedroom, then Ren and Frank Landusky undressed him and got him into the sickbed Libby had prepared. The presence of so many black-listed riders on an association ranch created an awkwardness they all felt. The faces of the Two C men were set in dark, deep scowls. Humanity and a hospitable instinct warred in Joe Garnet with feelings created by the sheep controversy. When there was nothing more to do for Gila until the Alkali doctor got there, Ren decided to relieve the situation.

Walking out to the yard, he said, "You boys go back to the roundup camp and get yourselves some sleep. We've done all we can, and I'll let you know as soon as I know anything more. And remember this. Goin' after Fowler and Jerome tooth and toenail won't help Gila a bit."

Their black looks had convinced him of how close they were to the raw edge of heedless violence. God knew he shared the feeling. It ate at his nerves and cut deeper and deeper into the restraints he had imposed on himself.

Libby had taken charge of Gila, but around noon she hurried out of the bedroom. "I think he's coming to," she whispered.

He hurried into the sickroom. Gila, who had been a dead weight so long, had turned restless. He turned his head from side to side and kept working his dry lips.

"Easy, boy," Ren said gently.

"Rita—"

Ren bent closer. "Don't worry about her now."

"She'll be—I'm her—only hope—" Gila's struggling lips

grew soundless, then ceased moving altogether. He had slipped into unconsciousness again.

Dr. Sprague, with his Two C escorts, got there from Alkali in the middle of the afternoon. A short, square-set man of middle age, he had grown thoroughly seasoned in the exigencies and crudities of a frontier medical practice. He needed only a summary examination of the wounded man to shake his head. Looking at Ren, he said, "I've got to go into that belly. If something's severed, in there, it's got to be repaired or he's got no chance. And I'll need help."

"Just name it."

"Tell Libby I want her kitchen. And her, to fetch and hand. You'll have to drip the chloroform."

The next two hours, in which he did what he was told as if his hands and body belonged to another person, were worse than any previous two years of Ren's life. Libby went through it, too, moving swiftly and competently, although when he glanced at her he could see how white she was. Yet those hours kept alive the flicker of hope. The bullet had done internal damage that, repaired, was not necessarily fatal. Gila was young and he was tough, with God alone knowing if that would be enough.

Afterward, when Gila was in his bed again, and the kitchen had been restored to order, Ren sat there with Sprague over scalding black coffee.

"You're apt to get a call to Crown or Fowler's place, Doc," he said. "At least two of 'em were hit, and maybe one was killed. Anyhow, they lashed him to a saddle to get him away."

"Your men reached me first, and I can't leave my patient here for the next few hours."

Sprague refrained from comment on the fight on the desert, although he knew the situation that had brought it about. His was a profession permitting no sides, between sheepmen and cattlemen, lawmen and outlaws, Christians and heathens. He went where called, did what he could, and kept a right rein on his tongue.

Ren went out to where his two punchers waited in the ranch yard. He told them there was no news to take to the roundup crew, one way or the other, but for them to go on. Gila was alive, that was all, and he had had the extra shock of a major operation. Afterward Ren stood watching them ride out through the fading afternoon. He couldn't remain here much longer, himself, but he was determined to do so as long as Garnet and Libby would tolerate his presence.

Late in the evening Gila took a turn for the worse, although all the others knew of it was a hint of worry the doctor could not conceal. Sprague stayed in the room with his patient, thereafter, and, around ten o'clock, Ren sprang to his feet when Garnet came out to the porch, where he sat half-dead in a chair.

Garnet had nothing to report, instead saying, "Ren, you and me're on the outs, ordinarily. But this ain't ordinary. The three of us've had sleep a lot more recent than you had any. Use my bed, and I'll stay up in case Doc needs help."

Ren glanced at him dully. "Thanks, Joe, but—"

"But me no buts, blast it. Get in there and catch some sleep. I'll call you if there's any reason."

To his surprise, Ren opened his eyes to broad daylight. He lay across the foot of Garnet's bed, where he had toppled the night before fully clad. The curtained doorway gave onto the kitchen, and when he walked out there Libby sat alone at the kitchen table. Her voice was kindly when she said, "You look better, Ren."

"How's Gila?"

"He had a sinking spell, last night, but he rallied. Dr. Sprague left a while ago."

"They call him over to the east basin?"

She shook her head. "He said there's a case in town he

had to check on. I hate to tell you this, but he also said there's nothing anybody can do here but wait."

Awkwardly, he said, "This is askin' a lot of you, Libby, the way you and Joe feel."

She gave him a penetrating glance. "Where else could you have taken him? The roundup camp—to headquarters—the hospital in Alkali? He'd be dead by now, if you'd tried. Besides, I want to take care of him. Gila and I were once good friends."

"Once," said Ren, "so were you and I."

She looked away. "I know. You go on, Ren. If Gila's to live, he'll need a lot of care. More than you and the boys could give him."

With a sigh, he said, "It could get Joe in mighty Dutch with the association."

"If you want my opinion," she said, still not looking at him, "I think the association's got in a little Dutch with him."

She insisted on giving him breakfast before he left. Afterward he looked in on Gila, but the man was either asleep or unconscious. With a sigh, he turned away, and ten minutes later was riding down Marsh Creek toward home range.

The men had come in to the chuckwagon for the noon meal. They had made a gather that morning, he saw as he neared, and were ready to start cutting it when they went back to work. His approach had turned them all toward him, like iron filings drawn by a magnet. Their silence, while he rode up, was a more eloquent question than any of them could have voiced.

"Well, I don't bring you bad news," was the best he could say. "It's still nip-and-tuck with Gila."

The small hope he had aroused died in their eyes, and the perpetual scowls they now wore deepened and darkened. Then Farraday broke a long silence.

"What if he don't pull through?"

"How do you mean?"

Vehemently, Farraday said, "They've outlawed and black-listed us. They've framed two of Lands' men into jail and drew a deadline across our own range. Now this, and you say not to carry the fight to them, for a change."

"Listen—"

"Hear me out. What if Gila don't make it? Could you swallow that, too?"

The puncher's impassioned outburst had expressed the feelings of them all. Ren felt the weight of the stern eyes that watched him and knew a dishonest answer would only make them despise him.

"No, boys," he said, shaking his head. "I don't reckon I could swallow it."

CHAPTER THIRTEEN

Rita held the curtain so it wouldn't blow and betray the fact that she was hidden behind it. She had chanced to be in the pantry, straightening up after breakfast, when Pearce Jerome stormed into the yard, where her father and the men were engaged in some kind of heated discussion. It was Roddy's saying, "Here comes old Pearce with his hackles up" that had made her linger by the open window to listen.

She knew that something terrible had happened on the high desert the night before, with an outcome that had made the men surly and insolent with her father. From the talk at breakfast, she knew they had been unhorsed and forced to foot it back, which affronted them more than it had taxed them physically. Her father had countered with his usual secretive indifference, telling them they hadn't seen the last of it yet. Afterward they had got in an argument in the yard. But she hadn't felt any interest until she realized the mighty Pearce Jerome had also been antagonized by Link Fowler.

"A fine kettle of fish!" Jerome bawled, when he pulled up outside. "So you're the smart aleck that could bring Two C to its knees in jig time!"

Fowler's voice drawled, "Simmer down, Pearce . . . It's better'n it looks, like I been tryin' to tell these lunkheads here."

"Better'n it looks?" Jerome exploded. "Seems to me you

handled Ren Tyler about the way you did at Massacre Pass when he stampeded your broncs! This time he set you down, by God, and half my crew with you! When that gets around, we'll be the laughingstock of the Hard Rock, and the association's finished!"

"Now, you hold on," Fowler cut in. "It don't have to get around. Nobody's having truck with Two C, these days. But if they try to spread it deliberately, we'll call 'em a bunch of liars."

"With one of my men dead and another shot through the arm? How're we gonna sweep that under the rug?"

Calmly, Fowler said, "Bury the carcass and say the fella drew his time and pulled stakes. As for a gunshot wound— hell, there's hardly a man on your payroll who don't know how to doctor one."

"Hide a killin'?" Jerome demanded. "I ain't goin' in for that."

"Then watch everything go out the window, and get yourself laughed outta the country, to boot."

Rita had absorbed many shocks in her day and was not surprised at the cold calculation with which her father sought to restore what apparently was a bad job on his part. Yet a sick, greasy mass had formed in her stomach while she listened. She wanted to turn away and not hear any more, but Gila had asked her to learn all she could from those callous men out there. She waited, her bare legs weak and trembling.

Jerome's voice was more moderate when it resumed. "Well, Roddy done a little better'n you, even if he did get chased home, too. Olie Elvek come out from Alkali, this morning. Couple of Two C punchers come in after Doc Sprague, last night. Seems their segundo got it in the belly at Two Fingers. A mean gut shot."

Rita felt herself swaying. That would be Gila—Gila. Her one friend, her only hope of escaping this and finding her baby. Shot in the stomach—that meant he might be dead already. The space about her began to darken, but she held onto a shelf and it passed.

"Who got chased home?" Hunk Roddy was saying in an angry voice. "If Link hadn't let hisself get suckered, I'd of wiped my bunch out."

Ordinarily Fowler would have flown off the handle at such a slur from one of his hirelings. His tolerance now showed his desperate need to restore the situation, to hold onto his command. He said mildly, "Go on. Let off enough steam, and mebbe you can see straight. Sure we got a setback. Who figured we could pull a stunt this big and not get one or two? They've got some smart hombres on their side. Who said they didn't? Just the same, I done what I set out to do last night." He laughed. "Ren Tyler can't halter them men of his much longer. Maybe not any longer. And once they go off the reservation, we've got 'em where we want 'em."

Jerome grumbled, "Damned if I see how."

"Them sheepers killed Meathead. Don't forget that. Nobody's gonna blame me and the boys for takin' that up for him. As for your part—all you gotta do is bury what's left of Val Baber and deny any part in it at all. But Two C knows better. They'll try to do to you the same as they do to me. After that, the association'll follow either of us to hell."

"You might be right," Jerome agreed. "If they do hit back."

"If Veyan's gut-shot, he's finished. And when he cashes his chips, they'll be after us. Me, you, or both of us."

Rita knew her father had won. After that their voices dropped to a more moderate pitch, and she could only make out parts of what they said. But she had heard too much already and turned away in an agony of despair and went back into the kitchen. They gave Gila no chance, and without him she had none, but that was not the whole reason for her terrible emptiness. She had liked Gila, ever so much more than she had realized in her obsessed preoccupation with the dead father of her baby. She wanted to see him, badly enough to defy the men in the yard and try to reach him, if there was a chance she could do so before he died.

But to do that would be to separate herself forever from her child.

Jerome left, and her father and his men cleared out of the yard, and she was alone with everything about her seeming cleaner again. The breakfast work was finished, and she did not need to start the noon meal for another hour. She went into her bedroom and sat down on the edge of her bed, staring at the blank wall. Something was changing in her. The thought of accepting this life, these conditions, a day longer was unbearable. And she had accepted them, abjectly, in her yearning to regain her child. If only she had some of the spirit that seemed to have taken Gila to his death. It was time she did something for herself.

Maybe there was a way to do it.

There was no man on the ranch she feared as much as she feared Hunk Roddy because of the way he looked at her sometimes when he thought no one was watching him. He harbored lust, and if anybody besides her father knew where the boy was being kept, it would be Roddy. She found herself trembling, revulsed by what she considered. She had to catch Roddy alone. That was the first step.

She tried at noon to catch his eye, but he was sulking, paying no attention to anybody. Later, when she put a fresh plate of biscuits on the table, she approached by his chair and let her hip touch him for an instant. She couldn't tell if he noticed it. That afternoon all the men left, and during supper she didn't catch Roddy looking at her once.

At twilight, she remembered how she had walked up the creek each evening, of late, hoping she might meet Gila. He could not come to her now, might never be here again, but she moved out into the yard mechanically. Her father was nowhere around, but she knew that the men were in the bunkhouse at their eternal cards. She lingered there a moment, then slanted off through the trees toward the stream. The spring air was warm, and there was hardly a cloud up above. At the creek bank she halted to watch the limpid water run over the rocks, its sound a chuckling conversation that had to suffice for Gila's voice. Then she went on up the creek to where she had met him.

The night began to fade, and nobody came from the other side of the ridge. She had not expected that, of course, but it had helped to imagine that someone would arrive to tell her that Gila would be all right. She turned to go in, and there he stood, watching her—Roddy.

Her blood hammered in her veins, and she heard its crash in her ears. She had invited it, but now that it had happened she was terrified. He came closer, but was still off a pace when he stopped uneasily again.

"Noticed how you take this little *pasear* of an evening," he said.

"I—I like a little air before I go to bed." Then, her voice lower, she said, "Where's my father?"

Roddy laughed. "Sure got you scared of gettin' caught with another hombre, ain't he? Never mind him. He went up to Crown."

She had to be arch, and it was like taking off her clothes with him watching. "Did Jerome get over his mad?" she asked, giving him a faint smile.

"So you heard the old wart hog give off head, this morning. Yeah, Link knows how to put his train back on the track. He does for fair." Roddy shook his shaggy head musingly, conveying a basic dislike of the man held in check by awe.

"Jerome's apt to be sorry a second time," she said mysteriously, still faintly smiling.

His eyes sharpened on her. "How come you say that?"

Encouraged, she said angrily, "You know Link Fowler

uses people. And he doesn't care a damn what happens to them, once he's done."

He pondered that, watching her awkwardly because he had fallen into her father's attitude of contempt and found it hard to meet her as an equal. "Strikes me he does," he said. "What made you say that, Rita?"

"Because you're all fools to trust him. If you don't believe me, get you a ouija board and ask Meathead."

"Meathead?" His voice grew stern. "What about him?"

"You know good and well who really killed him. Because Link Fowler wanted a good excuse for what you all did last night. Meathead trusted him. He'd of died for Link. And he did." Appalling as the thought was, she made herself laugh.

He came forward, and his hands caught her arms just above the elbows. He shook her. "You got reason to be sure of that?" he demanded.

Pulses battered her ears again, but she kept laughing. "You don't need a reason, Hunk. You know it because you know him, the same as I do."

"Yeah," he said, with a sound like a sigh. "I think I know it. But if I was real sure, I'd kill him. I liked that simple-minded kid, but it ain't the whole reason. I'd do it because it's what Link'd do to me, and for no more reason than that he found it useful to do it to me."

"Killing him wouldn't hurt very bad."

"What's worse?"

"Lots of things. One'd be losing his hold on me."

"Ah," he said on a long breath. "So you're tryin' to work me, too. Just like your old man."

"I'm not just like him, Hunk," she said angrily. "You know that good and well."

"You want somethin' of me."

"I'll pay for it." She nearly slumped and folded over when she said that. She didn't even know if it were possible for him to help her. Desperately, she said, "Hunk, do you know where my boy is?"

"So that's it."

"Do you?"

"Mebbe and mebbe not."

"Do you?"

"Could be."

He grinned at her, for he knew that he had a hold on her, himself. He knew, also, that to have his way with her he would need her assent, or he would be through here, with her father to deal with. That was all that protected her now from his merciless brute strength.

Her fear left her, and in its place she felt a strange, somehow triumphant calm. She said, "If you earn it, I'll pay, Hunk. Any way you say."

After a moment, he said, "Yeah, I guess mebbe you would. He's given you a mean time. Us boys never really thought you're as bad as he makes out. But that's how he wants it, and that's how it is."

"Are you teasing about knowing where little Wad—" But none of them knew the name she had given her baby, nobody but she and Gila. "About knowing where the boy is?"

He looked away. "I can tell you this much. The kid's all right."

"How big is he, Hunk?"

He held out a hand. "Dunno. About that tall, I reckon."

Her heart leaped. He had measured a boy of five. He must even have seen him recently, and the only place they went outside the Hard Rock was to California. But that covered an awful lot of territory. She could never narrow it down by herself. Even if she ran away and searched, her father would move the boy and keep moving him every time she got close. Roddy was her only hope.

But she hungered for everything she could learn of him,

of her child and Wad's. She said eagerly, "Is his hair still light?"

"Yeah. Regular towhead."

"Does he look like—?"

Roddy laughed. "His pappy? I'd say so. In a kid way." The man knew he was whetting her appetite, bringing her more and more into his power. "Blue eyes, as I recollect. Light and fast on his feet. Smart like, too. Learns quick. Real healthy young'un."

"A—a woman takes care of him?"

"Sure."

"Does he think—she's his mother?"

"I reckon he would. But look here. Next thing you'll want to know the kind of house he lives in and the kind of town, so you can go lookin' for him."

"No," she said hastily. "I only want to sort of picture him like he is now. It's been so long."

Night had closed about them fully. She still was not afraid of Roddy, any more, could never be again. He was a link between her and the son for whom she had lived. She almost liked him for being that. He had already given her more than her father ever would, some knowledge of and assurance about her boy. But her questions had already made him cagey. He was not going to tell her any more.

She turned and walked swiftly away from him, feeling his hungry eyes on her back. Apparently nobody had thought twice about Roddy's absence from the bunkhouse. The game was still going on in there. She turned toward the dark house and entered it and walked through the dark rooms to her own. She undressed quickly, got into her tattered nightgown, and crawled into bed.

Roddy gave her no least notice at breakfast, the next morning, leaving her with the terrible fear that he had decided the game was too dangerous for him to care to play it. In her panic she would have crawled to his feet and begged him to divulge the secret she must learn. It was the same thing during the noon meal, although she realized that, in her desperation, she was all but flirting with him openly. Only her awareness that this could make him withdraw completely enabled her to control and stop it.

When he did not follow her up the creek that evening, she gave up hope. He did not want her enough to run the risk involved.

The figure that approached her came from the other direction. She heard some sound and whirled and saw the shape of a walking man coming down through the creek trees from the west. She nearly cried out, thinking there had been some mistake, that it was Gila. Then the figure grew plainer, and she recognized Ren Tyler.

He didn't speak until he had come up to her, then he said softly, "Hello, Rita. Hope I didn't scare you. Gila couldn't come. He's—"

"Dead?" she cried.

"You heard? No, he's holding on, but that's all. He come to for a while last night. The only thing he was thinkin' of was you. I figured I ought to tell you that, and why he won't be showin' up, in case you didn't hear."

"They were talking about it yesterday. Will he—?" She couldn't complete the question.

"God knows, Rita, and only God. Gila's at Libby Garnet's. The doc patched him up the best possible. Figured I ought to come over and tell you. And it gave me something to do."

She put her hand on his arm. It was a strong arm. She could feel the ridges of muscle under the shirt. "Gila thought the world of you, Ren. I see why. If you ever can talk to him again, tell him I know where my baby is. In California somewhere. Roddy knows, and I made him tell me that much. Somehow I'll make him tell me the rest. And—and, Ren—"

"Yeah?"

"Tell him I was wrong in thinking Wad was the only man

I could ever feel that way about. I know it now. I wish Gila did."

"I'll tell him, Rita, if I get a chance."

He turned and was gone, which she knew to be wise for he would be dead in a minute if he was caught here, with herself in serious trouble. But he had restored her hope, her determination to do something for herself and be worthy of Gila's love, of a son like the boy in California.

"So big," she whispered, and held out a hand to see again for herself.

CHAPTER FOURTEEN

Knowing that the Garnets would send word when there was a change, for worse or better, Ren had repressed an overwhelming desire to ride back up Marsh Creek that night. But the urge to action drove him into the saddle after supper, anyway, and he had scarcely risen to leather when he knew what he would do. So he had headed east toward Turkey Neck and crossed, coming down to find Rita in the manner Gila had once described.

He rode slackly, his body not yet relieved of its accumulated fatigues, his mind heavy with his concerns. He was tempted to return to the roundup by way of Garnet's place, after all, in hope that Gila might be having another of those half-lucid moments. What Rita had told him about the child, especially what she had intimated about her own feelings, might be what the man needed to pull him through the crisis.

But the chance of being able to communicate with him again was too slight, and he rode directly down off Turkey Neck and entered the west basin. Dry Lake lay off to the south, its alkaline bed seeming to glow in the growing starshine. Spring had advanced far enough that the day's heat lingered, rendering up from the semidesert a rank and arid smell.

He rode at a trot across the basin floor, half-dozing, and when the lethargy passed he opened his eyes to see, off in the starlight, the winking fire of the roundup camp. The morning's gather had been cut that afternoon, and off to the left of the fire a puncher was holding the stray bunch. It was a peaceful, sleepy, familiar scene, and he didn't come fully alert until, as he neared the camp, he noticed that the night cavvy wasn't in its usual place.

An instant foreboding took him on at a faster pace. Only old Abe Jewett was at the camp, standing, watching, and waiting for him to arrive.

"Where're the boys?" Ren demanded.

Abe let out a gusty sound. "Halfway to Crown by now, I reckon. Ren, there was no holdin' 'em."

"What happened?"

"Joe Garnet was here a while after you left. Wanted somebody to go for the doctor again. Jim went, and Joe went back home."

"Gila—?"

Abe nodded. "He took a turn for the worse, Joe said. Fever and a fast heart. The doc told Libby them'd be bad signs. Somethin' about infection. Joe figured the doc should be brought again, even if it ain't any use."

Ren swallowed. "So the boys lit out for Crown."

"They don't have any hope Gila'll make it, and they hold old Pearce responsible. Without that lunatic, Link Fowler couldn't move out of his tracks. He just don't draw enough water."

"Why not Fowler's place?"

"His girl's there."

Ren swung away. He could have used a fresh horse, but all the night mounts had been taken. Since he had not caught sight of the men on the ridge, they must have crossed farther south, riding directly on the big Crown. He knew they were doing exactly what Fowler hoped, yet he could only sympathize with them. The emotions searing through him cried for action of the same kind. Reason and restraint had their good points, but there were times when a mere mortal could not command them.

He angled southeastward, this time passing the lower tip of sprawling Dry Lake, crossing thereafter the association's offensive deadline, and continuing on a sharp slant over the Pintos. Fortunately, his private horse had plenty of stamina and could still carry him rapidly. The stars told him it was somewhere around midnight when he topped over the summit. The east slope was open, gradual, and another half hour brought him in sight of an outsize glow of dull red flames, off below him. Reining in, he picked up the soft, grainy sound of shooting from the same direction.

There was no way to change things now, and this awareness eased the condemning twitches of his conscience. He went on down at a dead run, Crown's headquarters beginning to outline itself at the edge of the lagoon above the lake. It seemed to be one of the several outbuildings that was burning. So Two C must have set it, piling arson on assault, handing it to Fowler on a platter, yet somehow justified in venting their consuming anger.

He came in on the lighted edge of Crown, arcing around, then heading in on the blind facet of the fire. It was only an old shed that was burning, lighting up the whole near part of the ranch yard, bringing one wall of the house and bunk-house into bright relief. The shooting now rattling in his ears was more persistent than it was furious. All he could determine, from his present position, was that men were shooting through broken windows from the house and from the long, near-by bunkhouse. Two C seemed to be positioned on this side, rashly vulnerable to being surrounded and trapped.

He dismounted and began to make his way across the last distance, thinking Crown might have set fire to the building to light up the yard and its many hiding places. He hoped they had caught old Jerome inside, the man who was the fountainhead of all the poison. There was no estimating the number of riders caught here at headquarters. The association roundup had been due to start, and it always began far down the east basin, working across Cat Track and Pitchfork before it reached Crown.

He had moved through the last of the willows to the side wall of the smithy, when a low voice said urgently, "Ren— that you?"

"It's me."

Frank Landusky appeared in the side door of the shop. He murmured, "Seen somebody comin' from the meadow. Had you covered. And don't cuss us. Twenty-mule team couldn't have held the boys back, tonight. And me with 'em."

"Did I say anything? How many come?"

"Eight of us."

Two or three were between this point and the burning shed, which put four or five on the other side of the shop. He said, "Who set the fire?"

"Crown did and went to considerable work. Oil-soaked rags they set a match to, wrapped around rocks. Finally landed one in the straw on the floor. Don't know why the damned fools wanted to burn their own buildin'. Light hurts them as much as us."

If anything, Ren observed, it lighted the house and bunk-house more than it did the shadowed yard out from them. They could hardly have done it to forestall a rush, for the back sides of the buildings were still in the dark and vulnerable. But he was relieved that his men hadn't stooped to that.

Then all at once he saw their peril.

Crown was trying to draw help from Fowler's ranch down the basin! A fire like that could be seen plainly from down there. Meanwhile, Crown was fighting defensively, stalling to give the mustangers time to come in outside the line. If the horse outfit had noticed the fire at once, that could happen any time. The building must have burned fifteen or twenty minutes, and the horse ranch headquarters were only two or three miles distant.

Urgently, he said, "Frank, if we don't skedaddle, we're apt to be hanging by the heels like beef, come daylight. That's a signal to Fowler. It could have been arranged, in case either outfit got hit."

Landusky stared again at the nearly destroyed structure, then shifted his gaze northward. "By damn," he breathed. "Never thought of that."

"I don't blame anybody," Ren said tensely. "Comin' over, I was ready to pitch in, too. And it carried us into it, just the way they wanted. Know if Jerome's here?"

"Heard him yellin', at the start."

"He won't let us get away, if he can help. You tell the boys on the other side of the shop to start pullin' back, one at a time. Toward the horses, and mount up as fast as they get there. I'll see the men on this side."

Landusky nodded and faded around the corner of the building. The others, once they saw the logic of it, wouldn't be hard to persuade. Ren had to cross an opening, so he moved out a distance until he got a tree between himself and the house. There was still a little flickering light, which he crossed on the run, calling out softly to identify himself before one of his own men shot him.

He found Pete Farraday lying behind the wheel of a wagon and told him to get going. Watson was using the trunk of a tree for a breastwork. Ren sent him off and took his place, firing into the light-flickered wall of the big house. The shooting on the far side of the blacksmith shop died to that of a single gun. Ren's chest muscles tightened while he waited to see if the change brought Crown storming out of the house.

When nothing happened, he moved back to the side of the shop and fired twice more from there. Then he started to retreat. He moved slowly until the last man on the far side quit shooting, then turned, and hurried through the trees toward the open meadow.

The others had left their horses in the trees, a little down from his own. They were mounted except for one man, who was running toward them. Ren swung up, and as he hit leather, a shout carried from the house.

"Hey! They're pullin' out!"

He let his men ride up to him and rapped, "Too late to turn loose their horses. They'll be after us, sure. So we've got to make certain we don't run into Fowler."

"Over the Pintos?" Landusky asked.

"If we can make it."

"We won't find out if we don't try."

Although they rode at a clipping pound, it was apparent that men on fresh, fast horses could close the distance behind them. Their own had partly spent themselves coming over, while Ren's had made an extra trip to Fowler's ranch that night. They kept on the Crown lane for better going. When they reached its turnoff from the main road, which ran the length of East Basin, they pulled down to blow the animals.

Other horses were coming, although the worried men could see nothing behind them or to the north.

They waited as long as they dared, for the sake of the animals, then scurried on, leaving the road and entering the rough, scabrous and gully-washed plateau of the Pintos. The footing and climb combined to slow them further. Ren shifted in the saddle and twisted himself for a look back. That time he could detect a bunched party on the Crown lane. Only a moment later, Farraday yelled.

"Yonder's Fowler!"

It was true. A second party was streaking along the main basin road, coming from the north. The two bunches were aware of each other and planned to join, Ren realized. And since he could see them, they must by then have seen him and his men. There could be no sparing of the horses now. Two C whipped on up the grade.

They had nearly reached the first timber when Landusky's horse went end over end, tripped by a rock or hole.

The others swung as one man, wheeling and returning, dismayed. But Landusky scrambled to his feet, groggy and reeling, then the horse clambered up, limped a few steps, and stopped.

Ren extended a hand to the dumped rider. "Quick, Frank. Up behind me."

Farraday cut in to say, "Better let him double with me, Ren. My cayuse's got more bottom left than your'n."

"All right. Hurry."

A moment later they were speeding on, the lamed horse dropped behind, and the pursuit dangerously nearer than before. Gunfire began to dot the drum of hoofs, more a sign of blood lust than a danger, for the range was too great for effect. Two C's whole attention was on the timber ahead. It would be easier to throw them off, in there. Fringe trees soon breasted them, and, before they plunged deeper, the harried party wheeled to fling a shower of bullets rearward, to slow the other group and warn of trouble if it tried to follow into the forest. Then Two C hammered on. With the starshine cut off by the trees, they were slowed to a careful, way-picking walk, and a hundred yards within the woods, Ren signaled for another stop.

"We put a little fear of God in 'em," he commented. "They've got to allow for us making a stand at the edge of the timber."

"We better make one pretty soon," Farraday grunted, "or we're done for. These horses're pooped."

Ren shook his head. "No, if we go on, they'll figure we moved north toward home range. So we'll scatter and work south instead." He glanced at the man behind Farraday. "You all right, Frank?"

"Good enough."

"Then get going, all of you, and join up again at the narrows. If we shake 'em, they're not apt to come very far into our territory after us. That's risky, and they've already got what they wanted."

He knew the men hated this running from a fight, even from one in which they were themselves culpable, badly situated, and outnumbered. It was only to live to fight another day that they submitted and rode off through the timber to the south, slanting away from each other and giving their enemies no worth-while trail to follow even were it possible in the dark. Ren waited until the last of them had melted away. As he hoped, the pursuit had taken a cautious attitude about coming into the woods. He still could not hear them. He turned his horse and followed in the direction his men had taken.

He was soon far enough away he could afford to let his punished horse take its time. His men were so widely dispersed by then that he could see or hear nothing from them. The angle at which he traveled dropped him steadily and at last brought him out on the west basin floor.

To his relief, his slow gait had let all his men get there ahead of him. They were at the point where the town road came out of the wasp-waist gap between the two valleys on this side of the Pintos. They were dismounted, smoking, and Landusky seemed to have recovered fully from his bad spill. None of them had encountered trouble since separating, and they rode on in a group, reaching the roundup camp just as the tattered edge of dawn showed over Turkey Neck Ridge.

Ren waited to eat his breakfast, trying to calculate how long it had been since he really slept. Yet his weariness seemed to have resolved into a tense, brittle, nervous state in which feeling and even thought were dulled. No new word had arrived at the camp on Gila, nor could he take time to go over to Marsh Creek to inquire. Much had happened since his last report to Chance Abelard, who should be warned of the grim turn events had taken.

He roped and saddled a fresh horse from the *remuda,* then headed west, keeping the animal at a mile-eating lope. Around ten o'clock he swung down at the door of Chance's office and walked in. The handicapped man was there in his confining chair. His face was gaunt, older looking, giving Ren an inkling of what it was like to be physically helpless in a situation as potentially ruinous as this.

"Sorry I didn't get here sooner, Chance," he said. "And that even now I can only give you bad news."

Chance tried to smile and said, "Is there any other kind, any more? What now?"

Ren gave him a fill-in on Fowler's raid on the desert, Gila's wounding, and seemingly imminent death. Finally, without sparing himself and his men, on their heedless retaliation against Pearce Jerome the night before.

Chance said promptly, "I don't blame you a damn."

"Don't tell me you don't realize we asked 'em to strike at the heart of Two C itself. The association will rally to Crown, even if some don't like Fowler worth a damn. And Link seems to have his loop on Jerome for sure. That's the louse in the bedroll. Once Jerome wouldn't have stooped to things they've done of late."

"I know." Chance gazed out the window. He seemed more saddened than angry. "Fowler works on Pearce's vanity and prejudices, I suppose. They've blinded him so he can't see that Fowler's grinding his own ax. That Crown, itself, might eventually be his prey."

"None of us're gonna convince him," Ren reflected. "And the others don't seem to realize it. But what are we going to do? Ten to one they'll hit your headquarters before long, now that we hit theirs. The only way I can put men here to counter that is to stop the roundup."

Chance's eyes came back to him, troubled but cool. "Keep on with the roundup."

"Even if they don't get a fight here, which they'd like, they'll burn you to the ground. Another thing us boys asked for."

"If we let them paralyze us with fear, Ren, we soon won't need a headquarters, anyhow."

The lines of Ren's face reshaped into a weary grin. Rising, he said, "I don't wonder old Pearce come to hate you. If his life depended on it, he couldn't muster spunk like yours." He left to ride back to the roundup.

CHAPTER FIFTEEN

The first Rita knew of new trouble was when Roddy's urgent yell drew her father out of the house on the double. The latter had returned to the horse ranch shortly after her meeting with Ren, so she had retired to her room, undressed, and gone to bed. Then after she heard horses charge away, she had slipped out from under the covers, and, as she sat up, she grew aware of a vague brightness centered in the lower half of her open window. Hurrying to the window, she saw there was a fire far down the basin. More than once in her years there, a grass fire had taken the men off in a rush, like tonight's, and she had not realized the import of this one until later.

Somewhere after midnight, they had all come noisily into the house to get coffee, and from the snatches of talk she could make out through the partition she knew there had been another fight. They were laughing and cheerful, so she knew it had gone against Two C, this time, elating the men who had spoiled for revenge after the humiliating defeat on the high desert. The excitement in Roddy at breakfast, the next morning, showed her he was again wholly caught up in their pursuits. He ignored her as completely as if they had never had a personal and secret talk.

Somehow she had to manage to get him alone with her again.

Boldness was so unnatural to her instincts that she would

rather take poison than do what she had to, especially with a
man like him, but there was no alternative. She had a dress
she had outgrown long ago and put away, and before supper
that evening she donned it. Standing before her small, cracked
bedroom mirror, she nearly lost her heart because of the
way it accented the slimness of her waist and the flare of her
hips and breasts. If her father happened to notice he would
curse and foul her with names, and this might be the one
time he failed to regard her as another piece of furniture. Yet
she had to run the risk.

It went better than she had dared to hope. The men always
ate silently, wolfing their food, and this was especially her
father's way when he had something on his mind. He didn't
look at her the few times she had to replenish something
on the table. Since he sat with his back to the kitchen doorway, with Roddy across, the big foreman could watch her
enter and leave, and on her second trip she saw that he was
doing so. There was a change in his coarse, weathered features,
especially around his eyes. He was taking in every feature of
her figure.

She finished her kitchen work in the early dusk and was
tempted to change back to the loose calico she usually wore
before she went up the creek, for she had a strong intuition
that he would follow. But she had much to overcome in his
mind before she could have her way with him. She was
persuaded of his distrust, fear, and probable hatred of her
father. Entangled with that was his desire to be in on the
mounting trouble, and the spoils Link Fowler must have
promised the men.

Fortunately, her father had ridden off again, for Roddy
would never risk following her with him around. She kept
on the provocative dress and left the house, going to the
woodshed, but passing by it on the side away from the bunkhouse and slipping in among the trees. Roddy wouldn't have
to see her leave. He knew where she went and when.

She waited at her habitual haunt until well past dark, seated on a boulder and idly watching the lazy water. She was not worried by his failure to appear. He wanted the cloak of night about him, but he would come to her. She remembered that look on his face.

When he arrived, he simply loomed out of the darkness, hulking and motionless there by a tree. She felt the muscles tighten in her stomach as she sat looking toward him. She didn't know why he waited. Maybe he was listening for some foreign sound. When he came on toward her, finally, she did not get up.

He remained standing in that spraddled way of his, looking down at her. He offered no greeting, and there was complaint in his voice when he spoke.

"You know how to torment a man. Who taught you?"

Primly, she said, "I don't know what you mean."

"Don't give me that. No wonder Link keeps you out of sight. You could write your own ticket in a honky-tonk."

"I don't want to write my own ticket, Hunk. You know what I want."

He laughed. "It ain't me, I allow. It's to use me like Link does. You're another Fowler."

He was taking refuge in abuse, and she stood up so he could see her plainer. She pulled back her shoulders until her figure tightened against the cloth. Archly, she said, "If you're going to belittle me, I'll go."

"No, wait." She heard the noisy sound of his breath. "You been on my mind, Rita. I can't shake you out. But it's no good. There's a big thing comin'. Your pappy's gonna be top dog in the Hard Rock. It's what he wanted all along, and it's workin' out. Us boys'll have a big part in it."

"So he says," she answered scornfully.

"He's gotta have men like us. So why'd he cross us up?"

"Maybe he wouldn't. Trust him if you want."

"Well, I don't," he admitted. "I keep rememberin' Meathead. If a shot between my shoulders'd help Link, he'd put it there. Then help carry my coffin and bow his head at the grave. He's all sidewinder."

"If he gets what he's after," Rita encouraged, "how much do you really think he'll share with you and the boys? The land he grabs? The stock he steals? Come on, Hunk. You know you'll keep right on riding for wages."

"Well, a man's got to work," he said angrily, "when it comes to that. Can't live on woman fun."

"You're a top hand. You can get a better job easy, and live longer at it."

He glanced at her sharply. "Where do you fit into that?"

"Take me to my boy, and I'll stay with you afterward, as long as you want."

"In a pig's eye. You'd get what you want, and tell me to whistle for mine."

"Convince me of where he is, then, and I won't make you wait till you've delivered him."

His breath caught. "What if I convinced you right now?"

She shook her head. "I want more than your word. I don't more'n half believe you even know where he is."

Nettled, as she had hoped, he said, "I know, all right. I set it up for Link, back there."

"With friends of yours?" she encouraged.

"With my own sister. So do you think I know?"

She had wrung something from him, although she knew how little it was. What he said was apt to be true, since he had intimated at their other meeting that he had seen the boy not too long ago. But his sister might well be married, and could bear any of a million names, although she probably lived in some town they frequented or passed through when they delivered horses.

"If you're telling me the truth," she said.

Eagerly, he said, "I can take you to your kid, all right. That ain't sayin' I'm going to. There's somethin' coming up here in about a week I want in on. Not just to help your pappy. I got my own score to settle with Two C and Ren Tyler. We'll see how Link acts after that. If it looks like he's makin' snake tracks again, then, by God, I'll kill him. Then you and me'll light out."

She closed her eyes. At the very best, he was going to make her wait, hoping to save his cake and eat it, too. He wanted her. He would try to take her now, forcibly, if he dared. And being compelled to muster that much restraint, he could make himself wait as long as it was to his advantage. But she could not wait any longer. The torment of being almost in reach of her child was too great to bear.

She turned and left him, half running as she moved through the trees, trying to keep from crying. Her father had not got home. She crept through the dark, hot rooms of the house to her own, her private world, her whole world for so many years. Rebellion raddled her straining nerves. She could not, she would not endure it any more.

She must leave and search through every town between the Hard Rock and Sacramento City until she found Roddy's sister. She must accept the risk of her father's moving the child before she could succeed. The decision calmed her, and as her agitated thoughts quit swirling, she realized that the odds against her were not as great as they at first appeared. Not if she left immediately and went as fast as she could travel. Roddy had hinted that the big push against Two C was coming in about a week. That meant more to Link Fowler than she did or could, and he would not drop or even neglect it to pursue her. He would let that wait.

She heard him come home around midnight, and waited another hour before she slipped out of the house, taking nothing with her but the too tight dress she still wore. She paused in the yard to make sure the bunkhouse was dark and quiet, then moved down to the corral where the night horses were kept. She hadn't been allowed to ride, even under

guard, since the birth of the baby. But in her childhood her
father had taken pride in her skill with a rope and in the
saddle. She used it now, snaking out a horse she knew to be
a good one, fast and enduring. She saddled it, swung up, and
quietly rode away from her prison.

She was well up the creek, aiming for Turkey Neck Ridge,
before it came to her that, in her freedom, she could satisfy
another desire that lay enormous in her heart. It would cost
her time, but she could go by Joe Garnet's and see Gila,
find out if he still lived. Since the delay would put her father
closer upon her heels, in case he did pursue her at once, she
resorted to craft. Dropping into the creek, she rode in the
water until the roughening bed, at the edge of the ridge,
forced her out. Afterward she followed the ridge line until
she came to Forceps Creek, where again she entered the
water and remained until she cut the west basin road to
Alkali. There where travel had been heavier, she turned north
where any pursuer would expect her to go the other way,
toward California. Just before daylight, she arrived at Garnet's
place.

The shine of lamplight in a window was a moving reminder
that there was sickness in this house, but it meant at least
that Gila was still alive and there. She called out, as custom
required, then rode across the last distance and into the yard.
Her own purpose was forgotten in her quick and chilling
concern for the one man since Wad Wadsworth she could
think about without shrinking. She swung down, and as she
moved uncertainly onto the porch, she saw the light beyond
the door glass strengthen. Someone was carrying a lamp from
another room. The curtain kept her from seeing anything,
then a voice, a woman's, came softly through the panel.

"Who is it?"

"Rita—Rita Fowler."

The door opened immediately, and Libby stood there.
Although they had grown up within a few miles of each

other, they had never been allowed to get really acquainted. There was an expression of consternation on Libby's pretty features, and all at once Rita was embarrassed by her disheveled hair and revealing dress.

"Gila?" she gasped. "How is he?"

"About the same, Rita. Come in."

Libby moved back, and Rita followed her into the house. Libby crossed to a center table, put the lamp down, and turned around. She looked very tired. She said quietly, "Honey, did you risk it just to find out?"

"Not—entirely. I've run away. But I had to ask about him before I went on."

"I think you can do some good. Come with me."

She picked up the lamp again, and Rita went behind her to a bedroom whose scent warned her instantly of grave illness. For a moment the gaunt, bewhiskered man who lay in the bed didn't even resemble Gila. She stood staring at him, while Libby put the lamp on the dresser top and turned down the wick until the room was in thin, soft light.

"Gila," Rita whispered, and went over to the bed. "Gila."

She slumped down in the chair where Libby must have sat in long and lonely vigil, enormously grateful to her for that, but knowing that it was where she herself should be. Even if it meant giving up her chance to find her baby, she would not leave as long as Gila lay here like this. If somehow she could give him her own life, or will him to reclaim his own, she would do it.

She grew aware that Libby had slipped out of the room. She had to look close to tell that Gila's chest moved at all. Leaning nearer, she said softly, "It's me, Gila—Rita. I come to tell you I love you."

He seemed to have no ears at all.

Before she knew it, strong day had seeped into the bedroom. Gila had not moved a muscle in all the while she sat there. A soft voice had said, "Rita," and when, startled, she turned her head, Libby stood in the doorway, motioning for her to come. She rose and followed out and through another room into the kitchen. Joe Garnet was at the table, but he got to his feet and nodded.

He said, "Howdy, Rita. I hear you left the horse ranch for keeps. Your father know where you went?" She shook her head. "Well, I wanted to tell you we'll give you what help we can."

"I don't want to get you into trouble."

"We're already in trouble," he said bitterly. "This whole danged country's in trouble. Bad. We'll keep your horse in the barn, in case anybody spies on us from the rimrock. And you make yourself to home."

"Gila—?" she said weakly. "Has he got a chance?"

"Mebbe, if Libby's notion's sound. He nearly went, night before last, and we had to have the doctor out again. But he made it through that one, and the fever went down. You can spell Libby, which she won't let me do often, and I think mebbe you'll be good medicine for him. But first you need some breakfast."

She stared from one to the other. They were being kind to her, she realized, because they were made that way. An enormous gratitude warmed her heart, to them for being like they were, to God for creating them and giving Gila a fighting chance. She sat down where Libby indicated, not hungry for food but for their presence.

Garnet left for his work, and, feeling freer with the other girl, Rita said, "How long since you've been in bed?"

"Why, I've cat-napped, and my father's spelled me a lot, in spite of what he said. I was about to ask you the same question."

"Oh, I couldn't sleep," Rita said hastily. "Why don't you lay down a while?"

Libby was about to refuse, then something made her change her mind. "All right. As soon as I get the work done."

"I'll do it. You go on."

Again Libby looked at her hesitantly, then she went out.

Rita washed the dishes and swept the kitchen, steadying work that helped her forget her father and what he might do to these good people if he found out where she was. Afterward she slipped through the living room and sat down by Gila's bed. Sometime in her absence, he had turned his head her way. The face, darkened now by beard and deepened by pain, was frighteningly thin. She wondered how long he could live without eating anything.

She felt under the cover until she found one of his hands, which she drew gently to her. Then she sat holding it, feeling how hot and dry it was. Without conscious decision, she began to talk to him again.

"I know where my baby is, Gila. They took him to Roddy's sister, someplace in California, I think. I was just going to hunt for him, at first, but once I'd got away from there I knew I had to come to you. When I got here, I knew I had to stay with you. I don't really remember much about my baby, Gila. He's been gone so long, and from what Roddy said, I guess he's in good enough hands. He's five now, and he looks like his father. I still want to see him, but you're the one who counts now. I never thought it would happen again, but I love you."

She didn't know how long it was after that when his hand began to grip hers. At first she wasn't sure, but over a period of time it perceptibly tightened. After a while, it almost hurt her own, but she didn't try to withdraw. The vacant strain seemed to be leaving his face. When presently she saw the increased depth of his breathing, she could have cried out. Before her very eyes he had made the transition from torpor to normal sleep.

She wasn't aware of her strained position until Libby's hand fell on her shoulder. When she glanced up, the other girl was smiling. She looked greatly rested, so considerable time had passed.

"Honey, you've done it," she said softly. "Look at the color in his face."

"He never knew I was here," Rita said.

"I'm not at all sure of that."

CHAPTER SIXTEEN

Fowler was halfway through the kitchen before something strange about the room split his attention. He took another step toward the back door, wanting to wash his sleep-hot face, and then the other part of his mind turned him about. It was not so odd that Rita was not in the room. But what he had noticed, he realized, was that there was no breakfast fire going. The stove was stone-cold. It was the first time she had failed to have the morning meal started when he got up since he had turned the cooking over to her.

Angered, he swung back and walked noisily into her bedroom. At the doorway he hauled up, his gritty eyes widened. The bed was empty. It hadn't even been slept in. He stared in amazement while his yeasty temper took on a deep tinge of fear.

Some man again, and this time she had run off.

He jerked down the few cheap dresses in the curtained corner closet and trampled them underfoot. He ripped the yellowed mirror off the wall and smashed it over the foot of the bed. Then he overturned the box where she kept her trinkets and splintered the box with a vicious kick. He grabbed the footboard of the bed and shook it until that end of the bed came down. Then he wheeled and went striding out of the house.

At the corral he discovered which horse was missing, which saddle, and from there he went stumping to the bunkhouse to find out which man, if it was one of them in spite of only one horse's being gone.

The men were all there, a couple scrubbing at the wash bench, the others getting dressed. Roddy was fully clad and rolling the cigarette he had to have as soon as he got out of bed. He stared toward the doorway where Fowler stood, his tongue still on the paper he was licking.

Fowler growled, "Come here," and turned back.

The foreman followed him into the yard, and Fowler kept walking until they were out of earshot. Fowler planted his hands on his hips and demanded, "Who's been snoopin' around while I was gone and relyin' on you to look out for things here?"

Roddy's scowling face darkened. "You better cut the deck again, Link. What's wrong?"

"Rita skinned out. Sometime last night."

Roddy's head ducked forward, and his mouth opened. "Hell she did. Sure?"

"The piebald's gone, and the saddle she used to use. Bed ain't been slept in. She's gone, all right. And what son of a bitch towed her off?"

"Man?"

"What else'd make her give up her chance to get back the results of the last one?"

"Ain't been no man sneakin' in here," Roddy said with emphasis.

"Then what?" Fowler began to divine an alternative, himself, because of some vague, hangdog twist on the foreman's face. He said explosively, "You tell her where the kid is?"

"Why the hell would I? Damn it, Link, this is news to me, too. Instead of jowerin' about it, we ought to go after her."

"We?" Fowler snorted. "You think I want it spread over

the basin? I'll go after her, and I'll fetch her back. And, by God, I'll find out what got into her."

"Better get some breakfast, first."

"Hell with that. Saddle my horse."

Fowler went back to the house to strap on his gun. Ten minutes later he was mounted and had picked up his daughter's sign. It puzzled him why she had turned up the creek toward Turkey Neck, when the east basin road to Alkali would have been shorter for her. If that was where she was going, on her way to California. If it wasn't a man, it had to be her boy. Those were the only things she cared about.

He reined in, somewhat later, when he found she had entered the water. Had he been anything less than outraged, he might have admired her for that. When she was small, before men took to noticing her, he had taught her a lot of range craft. It seemed she remembered it. But she could not have stuck with the stream bed very far, and all he had to do to determine which side she had emerged on was to ride both sides as far as the ridge. He remained on the present bank and went on at a trot. Where the creek bed roughened, he grinned thinly. It wouldn't be necessary to ride the other side. She had come out on this bank and struck off up the slope.

He scarcely slowed, later where she turned south along the crest of the ridge. That was more like it, and she had resorted to the shenanigans in hope of throwing him off the scent. Yet after a couple of miles he lost the sign and had to double back and circle to discover that she had turned down Forceps Creek. She was trickier than he had allowed, and he grew less confident of overtaking her as speedily as he had estimated.

The next hour finished restoring his baffled desperation. She had stuck with the creek all the way to the west basin road, and could even have gone on down to where the stream ended in a dry sink. It was more likely, though, that she had turned toward Alkali to lose her tracks in the heavy scuffing along the road. He paused at the ford to make and light a cigarette. She had left quite a while before he discovered it, for there were no damp tracks to show where she came out of the water.

The tobacco tasted bitter, and its flavor seeped into his mind. He had gone to bed the night before convinced that he had the setup he had dreamed about for years. He had told Jerome to call a rump session of the association, and it had been held at Crown that evening. He hadn't had time to tell his own men what had been decided there, but they knew what he had hoped to put over. Had Rita, in her silent, unnoticed way, learned more than he had realized? Was that why she left, to curry favor with his enemies in an effort to gain their help? If so, it would hamper him and even hurt his chances, for much rested on letting Two C grow slack again so it could be caught off guard.

As his displeasure increased, he discerned dangers deeper and greater yet. If, carelessly, he or one of his men had let her guess his real and secret plan to take over West Basin for himself, the association would turn on him like wolves. He had Jerome in his power, now, but had had to harangue the others, fanning their resentment of the attack on Crown. But finally he had convinced them that Chance Abelard and Two C had to be destroyed in a once-and-for-all fight, and the date had been set for a week from that night.

Reminded of all that, and seeing a new possibility for Rita's leaving, Fowler realized that, at the rate he was going, he could not take time to track her southward while the scent was still warm. Even if she managed to find the boy, Roddy's sister wasn't apt to turn him over to her on Rita's say-so. But he could ride a piece toward Two C's roundup or head-quarters, instead. If he picked up her sign again, he would know for sure what she had done and where she was and could guide himself accordingly.

He swung the horse and crossed the ford. Then abruptly
there fused in his mind two reasons why his daughter could
have run away from home. A man and revenge, both achieved
with one stroke. Gila Veyan. He had been a friend of
Wadsworth's, a fact that had always made Fowler uneasy in
his presence. He had quit the horse ranch in bitter anger
after Wadsworth's death.

So maybe he had struck back through the girl, sneaking
in under everyone's nose to see her. Maybe he was even
gone on her, himself. That was where she could have headed.
To Joe Garnet's where, Fowler had learned, Veyan had been
left after he was wounded on the high desert. Fowler knew
he would pay a little visit there, himself, before he looked
anyplace else.

His hunch was so strong he didn't bother to hunt for her
sign along the road. Nor, at the fork, did he pay any attention
to the branch that curved off into the smoky distance toward
Two C's domain. He rode swiftly and thus, in about an hour,
raised Garnet's headquarters in the foreground. He went
directly in, not announcing himself, in hopes of taking the
people there off guard.

He had grown sufficiently calm to be pleased when Libby
came to the open door and glanced out. A shock she could
not contain pulled her pretty face out of shape for an instant.
That told him little, for he understood her chronic fear of
him. He decided to play a little cat-and-mouse with her,
and touched his hat in accentuated respect. She failed to
respond, even so, and he swung down and came up the
steps toward her. He had a feeling she wanted to slam the
door and lock it.

One of these times, he thought, when he was the big man
in the Hard Rock, she might change that persnickety attitude.

He said, "Howdy, Libby. Wonderful morning, ain't it?"

She swallowed, then said, "What are you doing here?"

He laughed. "Just hankered to see you, Libby. Since that

big Two C ramrod don't come around here any more, I figured mebbe you were lonesome." He kept on toward her.

"Stop right there, Link," a voice said behind him. "I got a gun on your back."

The unstable temper that had roweled Fowler all morning went out of control again. He knew Joe Garnet's voice. He wanted to whirl with a fisted gun, but some lingering common sense warned him. Garnet was quiet, soft-spoken, usually. But he never backed down from a stand.

"Turn around," the voice said, "and climb back aboard that horse."

Fowler swung slowly around, his hand conspicuously wide of his gun. Garnet stood below the steps, and the gun in his hand never wavered. The eyes above them were as pointedly cold as the tips of icicles.

"She asked a question," Garnet said. "What'd you come here for?"

Furiously, Fowler said, "You know damned well what I'm here for. My girl. And I aim to have her."

He expected Garnet to deny that she was there, to try to confuse the issue. Instead, the man said, "You're not gonna get her, Link. Now, tomorrow, or ever. The way you've used that girl's a crime. The way none of us ever did anything about it is another. You wanted a deadline, so now I'm gonna draw one. Between your spread and mine. After this, stay on your side."

Fowler said intensely, "I can crack your hardscrabble outfit across my knee any time I choose! And one of these days I'll do it!"

"You're not telling me nothing," Garnet retorted. "I've wondered quite a spell if it wasn't your idea to take over me and a lot of other little fellas, along with Two C."

"So you've gone over to their side."

"Two C's? I never said that. I just ain't on yours, and I never was."

"By God, I'll get you, Joe. Don't think I won't. You're way outta bounds harborin' a man's own runaway girl, and don't think I aim to let you keep her."

A third voice spoke behind him, one that shot excitement through Fowler, for it was Rita's. "No. I'll go with him, Mr. Garnet."

Fowler turned to look at her. She had come up behind Libby in the doorway. Her cheeks were empty of blood, but her eyes held something he had never seen there before. It dawned on him that this was courage.

With a short laugh, he said, "That's more like it. Wherever you stashed her horse, Joe, fetch it. Pronto."

"Not any."

Desperately, Rita cried, "Please, Mr. Garnet, I don't want to cause you trouble."

"Go back indoors, Rita. You, too, Libby. And, Link, you get on that cayuse and make tracks. Think twice about comin' here to take her by force. You don't know how this country despised you after you killed Wadsworth and took her child away from her, and the way you done her ever after. Every ambition you've got'll go hell a-hikin' if you do a thing more to her now. Don't you mistake it."

Fowler's mouth gaped open. That was so true, he wondered if he had lost his reason with his temper when he made those naked threats. The big plan had to be brought off before he could do anything about this situation. Wordlessly, he stalked down past Garnet and mounted his horse. Without another look at them, he rode off.

It was noon when he got back to the horse ranch, and it galled him to see the men loafing there, although at present he had no work for them to do. They drew his pay and were a force he had assembled for a long range, as well as an immediate, purpose. For more reasons than one, he had to speed things up.

They looked at him curiously while he rode through the

yard and stopped at the corral. He ignored them, and only Roddy followed him to the gate.

"Give up?" the foreman asked.

"I know where she is," Fowler snapped. "And she'll keep."

"Link, you ain't harmed her?"

"Harmed her?" Then Fowler laughed. "You mean, did I catch her in the timber somewhere and shoot her? What's the matter, Hunk? You kind of soft on her?"

Angrily, Roddy said, "By God, there's a limit to what a man'll take. She ain't a trollop, though it's a wonder, the abuse she's had from you."

"So," Fowler mused. "First Meathead, then you, huh? How long's this been goin' on?"

"There's been nothin' between us. And when it comes to Meathead—" The big man broke off.

Softly, Fowler said, "What about Meathead?"

"Never mind."

Fowler knew Roddy understood more than he had let on about that affair, and he didn't care a damn. Let them distrust and fear him, it would only make them more obedient. He walked up to the house, where a couple of the men had roustered a meal. The rest had eaten, so he sat down with a plate of food, lost in his thoughts. By the time he had smoked a cigarette and finished his coffee, he knew he would pay another visit to Crown.

A hot spring afternoon was well along by the time he drew in sight of Jerome's headquarters. The association roundup had moved on to Crown, now, and the old fellow might be down there watching the work. But it would be well to check at headquarters before making the extra long ride, and Fowler turned off the road onto the lane.

Since he wanted a private talk with Jerome, he was pleased to find him at the big house, looking over some new tally figures. When he saw who had come in, Jerome's face darkened. He had never been able to hide completely his distaste for this relationship, but that had not bothered Fowler, nor did it now.

"Pearce," Fowler said, helping himself to the chair across the desk from the old man, "we're gonna move the fireworks ahead a few days."

Jerome's old eyes grew piercing. "Ahead? What for?"

"Mainly because I want it settled."

"Because you want—" Jerome's mouth dropped open, and he fell silent. After a moment, he said, "Now, you look here, Link. Seems to me I never see you, any more, except to get your orders. We settled when it's gonna be, and it stays that way."

Fowler shook his head. He was spoiling for trouble with almost anybody, and now was an excellent time to set Jerome straight on a few things. "We move when I say we move, Pearce. The only reason I bother with you is you've got to give the orders."

"And what makes you think I'll take my orders from you?"

"I don't think it, I know you will. You forgotten Val Baber, that rider of your'n that was killed on the high desert? Ever report it to the sheriff?"

"No. You said—" Jerome's face sagged. "Damn it, you dug a pit for me with that. Bury the body, you told me. Say he drew his time and left the country. So that's what I done."

"Sure be a stink if the truth come out now," Fowler drawled. "Mebbe you could make the law believe you didn't know what really happened. Again, mebbe you couldn't. And that's a mighty serious charge, Pearce. Coverin' up a killing."

The old man looked stupefied and just sat there, dumbly shaking his head. Presently, he said, "What're you gonna do afterward?"

"Leave that to me," Fowler snapped. "All you gotta do is not interfere."

"I can't let you turn on the people we've talked into this, which is what you're fixing to do. Two C's one thing, but the others—" Jerome went back to shaking his head. He knew he was hopelessly caught.

Fowler grinned, reminded of some of the wild horses he had trapped and tamed. In his mocking, silky way, he said, "Who said I was gonna turn on 'em? At least, on all of 'em?" He laughed, then his eyes hardened. "You get the word out. I want everybody here tomorrow night by dark."

"What's your rush?" Jerome said on a surge of rebellion.

"That tramp I've supported all these years skinned over to Garnet's, and he stood me off with a gun. He's got influence with the other little fellas. If we give Joe time, they're apt to be fighting for Chance Abelard, not you. How'd you like that?"

CHAPTER SEVENTEEN

Joe Garnet felt saner, cleaner, while he watched Fowler ride away, although below this was another new feeling, one of inutterable dread. The vague nagging had grown ever since Rita's arrival in the late night. It had kept him close to headquarters, after breakfast, or she would have been taken away by force. He knew he had only baffled the mustanger temporarily. And the time was close when nothing could avert the full force of his wrath.

He didn't know Libby had joined him on the porch until she spoke at his elbow. "I'm proud of you, Dad. That's probably the first time anybody in the Hard Rock ever told Fowler what he thought of him. Outside of Two C, at least."

"Don't lump me with Two C," Garnet said testily. "Not likin' Fowler's stink don't make me *muy amigos* with them. This ruckus started over sheep, and that's still what it's over, in spite of Link and his schemes."

"Do you really believe that's all it is with Jerome?"

"Well, no," he admitted. "Pearce has let old grudges influence him. But he ain't a man us little fellas need to fear. Nor the kind that'd set by and let Link take us over."

"You hope."

Garnet glanced at her sourly. She was the apple of his eye, but it graveled him the way she could see things he tried to hide from her, even from himself. Put to it, he wasn't sure which of the two big operators he would rather trust, Jerome or Chance Abelard, sheep or no sheep.

She laughed and said, "Gila's a lot better, and it's Rita's doing."

"He is?" Garnet said, relieved that she had let him off the hook.

"Sleeping like a baby and nearly as pink-cheeked. You ought to ride over and tell Ren and his men."

"Yeah, I ought to," Garnet said readily. "And I can about catch 'em at the camp for noon, if I hurry. I don't reckon we'll see Fowler again till he's free to concentrate his meanness on us."

"There's something else Ren ought to know," Libby said. "Rita just told me. She found out that Roddy knows where they took her little boy. She tried to tempt him to run away with her, with the boy her price. Roddy stalled. He said something was going to happen here in about a week that he wants a part in."

"The big push," Garnet said dismally.

She nodded. "And Ren should be told."

Garnet knew that was so, although he didn't want the job of telling him. The smartest thing for him, Varley Eden, and the other small operators, was to climb on the fence and stay there and hope for the best. But with Fowler calling the dance, his conscience would condemn him forever if he didn't warn Ren and give him a chance to get set.

He said gruffly, "When'd she hear this from Roddy?"

"A while before she left, last night."

"A week from now, then. Well, I ain't gonna let Ren's bunch get caught and butchered."

He knew his decision pleased her, and he knew also that she was still in love with the Two C ramrod. Maybe she had even come around to his way of thinking, although Garnet himself never could. He saddled a horse and rode off down Marsh Creek, seeing across the distance the association strays

Ren had sent to him to be returned to the proper owners when the roundup got here. He had to allow that that had been fair dealing. But sheep were sheep, and bringing them into the Hard Rock deliberately was as unforgivable as the importing of Texas-fever ticks.

Garnet knew of several areas that had been scourged by the hoofed locusts. It had happened a lot in the early days, when tramp sheepers, out for a killing, came over from California and grazed off all the grass in sight, leaving devastated range behind them. That was still the principle in this fight, even if the fighting had turned out be different than some of them had expected. A man might trust Chance Abelard, but he couldn't be sure of others that his venture, if successful, could encourage to enter the country.

As he had calculated, Two C was nooning when he rode in to the roundup camp. He skirted the herd that waited to be cut and went on to the wagon to find that they had been watching toward Marsh Creek a long while, hoping for news from Gila. They had been eating, but nobody was now, for they all had their eyes glued to him.

"Well, boys," he said with satisfaction, "he's over the hump. Fowler's girl run off and come over, last night. I reckon she was just the medicine Gila needed."

He grinned when one of the punchers tossed his plate, food and all, into the air and let out a wild, delighted yell. Soon they were all on their feet, shaking hands, clapping each other on the shoulder, noisy, happy about it.

"Light down, Joe!" Ren called in gusty good humor, "and spear a bean with us!"

"Gotta get home," Garnet said, not wanting them to read too much into his coming, "but I'd like a word with you, Ren."

"Sure thing."

They moved out a distance from the camp, and there Garnet reported what Libby had learned from Rita of Fowler's intentions, concluding, "Don't get me wrong. Me buckin' his brand of dirty business don't mean I've changed my mind about things. And I ain't apt to."

Ren shrugged. "Man lives by what he's learned, I guess. Can't say I blame you. But I'm sorry so many in the Hard Rock quit learnin' sometime ago and don't care to bother, any more. Thanks for telling me, Joe. We knew it would come, and it sure helps to know about when."

Garnet nodded and moved out on the ride home, toying with the idea of calling a little meeting of his own, involving the small fry in the Hard Rock. Conceivably, he might even get outfits as big as Cat Track, Hat, and Hay Fork to sit it out and let the Fowler-Crown contingent fight it to a finish with Two C. United, they could form a third power in the Hard Rock, strong enough to command respect. If he could get them to assemble at his place, maybe Rita would help convince them that they were in more danger from Fowler than from Two C. At least he could ride around in a day or two and feel out a few of them.

Libby would expect him to eat at the roundup camp, which his stiff-necked pride had kept him from doing, and there were chores he had neglected all morning. Although he was a trifle hungry, he spent the afternoon at them before he went in. And when he reached home, it was to find a scene almost of gaiety.

Rita had slept, finally, and afterward had washed her hair and accepted the loan of one of Libby's dresses. Garnet blinked at what a beautiful young woman she was. He soon learned what had prompted the primping. Gila was awake and had eaten a bowl of soup, the girls told him. When Garnet went into the sickroom, he was astounded by the improvement in the patient.

Dryly, he said, "If I had a girl as pretty as Rita, bedamned if I wouldn't shave my whiskers."

Gila was still weak, but he grinned. "Give me time, Joe.

I'm glad you come in. Been wantin' to thank you for letting me be here."

"Didn't cost me much but the space you took up. Libby done the work, with Rita helping her lately." Garnet was embarrassed. He liked this puncher and always had, and down in his heart he knew he still liked Ren Tyler and even Chance Abelard. It was unsettling to have his feelings get in the way of his head.

"Libby told me you went over to the roundup," Gila said.

"Yeah."

"How're they doing?"

"Fine. Didn't you figure they could, without you?"

"Don't see how."

Garnet felt better, himself, than he had in quite a while. He relished his supper and, afterward, enjoyed his pipe while he sat on the front porch. He was more drawn than ever to his idea of uniting the little outfits into a third bloc, dedicated to nothing but self-preservation. It was too late tonight, but tomorrow he would ride down and talk to Varley Eden. It was quite a trip, and if Varley were interested, he could stay overnight, and the next day they could go on south and see some of the others.

He left around three o'clock, the next afternoon, and reached the little ranch at the narrows in time for supper. Eden was getting along in years and was inclined to be testy, and Garnet knew he might be a hard nut to crack. So he waited until Varley had his belly filled comfortably before he explained his visit.

Eden took it impassively, almost skeptically, and sat smoking a few minutes after Garnet stopped talking. "Well," he said, knocking out his pipe on the porch railing, "I reckon Link meant everything he threatened you with. I'm one of them that kicked over the traces about lettin' him have so much say in the association. What's a wild-horse hunter, with hardly any range of his own, doin' in a cattle association?"

"This one's tryin' to get himself some more range. Plenty of it."

"Likely," Eden conceded. "But you know good and well old Pearce wouldn't stand for that. He ain't a crook. And he's never run over us little fellers. You know that, and you just let Fowler spook you."

"Mebbe. But he's springin' somethin' on Two C that I don't like the looks of."

Eden glanced at him shrewdly. "That's right, you wasn't at the last meetin'. I was. And it ain't Fowler that's springin' it. It's the entire association. Official, and it's got old Pearce's blessing."

"But what's it to be?"

"They never told us anything except where to meet and when."

"You ridin' with 'em?"

"Nope. I'm beholden to Chance for favors. But I ain't helpin' him, either. He ain't backed down a inch on that stinkin' sheep business. Hoped he would before it reached this stage, but he seems bound and determined to bull it through. So what happens is his own fault."

Discouraged, Garnet said, "How about the other little fellas?"

"They're all rarin' to go."

That knocked the last prop from under his design. Wearily, Garnet said, "Well, I hope something happens the next few days to change their minds."

"Next few days? Blazes, man, it's for tonight."

Garnet's back straightened. "Tonight?"

Eden nodded. "They set it ahead. Burt Ames come over this mornin' to tell me, but I still ain't takin' a hand in it."

Garnet's belly muscles had gone hard as a slab of rock. He had himself told Ren it wouldn't happen for a few days more. Ren would think he had done it deliberately to deceive and disarm him. He shoved to his feet, staring vacantly across the growing dusk. Even with hard riding, he couldn't reach the roundup, from there, under two hours. Meanwhile there was no one at Two C headquarters but Chance and the handful of men who did the work there. He could reach headquarters in a little less time, and that was where the raiders were most apt to strike. . . .

"Leavin' so soon?" Eden was saying.

Garnet was nearly as astounded as Eden at the words that spilled off his lips. "You and me're fools, Varley, to think a man can set on the fence at a time like this. They're fightin' our fight, and if we don't pitch in, we'll drag our tails ever afterward."

"You want in on it? They was to meet at Crown before dark. Likely be over this side pretty soon. You might join up then."

"I want in on it," Garnet said vehemently. "And I'm headin' for Two C right now."

"Hey—"

"Don't try to stop me, Varley, without a gun."

"I won't try to stop you from committin' suicide. It's your privilege."

Five minutes later, Garnet was riding north at a gallop, knowing he had worked pretty hard to hold onto his blind bias. With the showdown right on top of them, he knew he would rather trust his fate in it to Chance Abelard than to any of the others.

Night ran in swiftly, and shortly afterward he stopped to blow the horse for a moment. It was then that he heard the sound of another coming along the road behind. He had reached the first marshes, and now he swung off the trail to press into the fringing brush. He could still see several hundred feet down the road and waited with his six-gun gripped. His eyes widened and his lips rounded when he recognized Eden. The man had a rifle balanced across his lap. Garnet couldn't credit that he was going to try to stop him from warning Two C, after all.

He rode out just as Eden came abreast, his gun ready, yelling, "Hold up, Varley!"

The other horse slid to a stop as Eden brought it around. He had lifted the rifle, but only to hold onto it, and his gaze went to the pistol in Garnet's hand.

"Stick it back in the leather," he said.

"Where you goin'?"

"Same place you are. Seein' you move so fast sort of jolted loose some stuck thoughts in my own head. Like how I'd rather have Chance and his sheep than Pearce and his mustanger, any time. Let's rattle our hocks."

Eden did not know the exact location of the roundup, but he could find the headquarters with his eyes shut. Garnet decided to send him there with the warning, and hit for the camp himself.

They had reached Two C's hay land, which the headquarters road cut across. Garnet waved Eden on and continued in a due-north course up the basin. From what the other had told him, he knew the odds would be heavily against the side with which he had cast his lot. But he was settled about it. Sometimes a man never did much honest thinking until the chips went down, and he was forced to do it fast. It had been the same with Eden, both of them going on custom and bias until the pit yawned under their very feet. He hoped enough of the others would have the same reaction to give Two C a fighting chance.

Urgency hounded him, but he had sense enough to know he needed sound horseflesh under him and presently reined in again for a short rest. It was then that he saw the strange glow far to the rear, almost down in Eden's own hay meadow. He sat scratching his jaw and scowling as he stared through the night. The glow enlarged. It was a fire, all right. The night riders had reached the basin, or some of that bunch had come on ahead.

Suddenly he saw through it. They were burning Eden's hay crop to create a diversion. They expected the holocaust to draw the Two C crew from the roundup and take it off down there, while the main raiding force hit at the ranch's headquarters and heart. Fowler's doings, a cynical use of Eden, who belonged to the association and had believed in and trusted it. Garnet was glad his friend had not waited for this to see the need to change sides.

He rushed on. Two C would notice the fire well before he could reach the camp, and he might not be able to intercept and turn it toward the place it should go. There was as yet no moon, no stars, and he could see only a few hundred feet, while the tattoo beat up by his horse kept him from hearing much else. The best he could do was ride awhile, then stop for a moment to listen.

He had done this twice before he heard them, his heart sickening. They were over on his left and either abreast or already behind him. With a groan, he sat trying to fix their position in the darkness. Then his head cleared, and, pulling his gun, he fired three shots in the air, the chance slight that they would detect them in the sound of their own rushing horses. There was no change in the distant beat of hoofs. He fired the other three shots, and it was the same thing.

They were bearing on the fire, now large and distinct in the far south, and if he did the same he would eventually intercept them. That would cost time, but if he didn't take it, the headquarters, and maybe the men trying to defend them, would be destroyed before Ren discovered the trick.

He sent his horse driving toward the distant red daub, and, riding with the reins hooked over the saddle horn, reloaded his gun. He no longer stopped to listen and trusted the animal to make its own way through the darkness. Moments passed that seemed hours, and then he raised them, ahead and slightly off to his left.

This time, when he fired into the air, they heard and hauled about, not knowing what it was. He waved his hat as he rode toward them, but even so they stirred defensively. Then the distance narrowed enough for them to hear, and he shouted his identity. They came back to meet him.

He told them in a strained voice what he had learned at Eden's ranch and what he believed.

In a bitter tone, Ren said, "You're right. But that fire's gonna spread into our hay. Next winter's feed." Then the shock left his voice, and he rapped, "Frank, you and Flint go on to where the road cuts across and set a backfire. Too late to do Varley much good, anyhow, and it might save our crop. The rest of you come with me."

CHAPTER EIGHTEEN

They rode the edge of the extensive marsh of Crank Creek, which so long ago Chance had conquered and turned into a fertile producer of hay for his beef. A crop swayed there now on the gentle breeze, all but ripened. It was as inviting to the night raiders as that of Varley Eden, now burning in a massive red sea, deep in the southeast.

Each time they halted their headlong rush to look back, Ren hoped to see the backfire he had told his men to set. Nothing disclosed itself against the glittering brightness off there. Maybe the backfire was drowned out by the much greater conflagration. Or maybe the Two C men had run into trouble before they could get it started.

A year ago, no one could have foreseen that Two C would have to defend its headquarters against the entire Hard Rock. The problem it posed was overwhelming. Ren's gaze fixed on the spur of the Kettles that ran out on the basin floor, a dark, digitate mass in the starshine that at last was emerging. Crank Creek's valley lay beyond, a tongue of the basin floor that ran into the Kettles for several miles. Just out from the debouch, and at the tip of the point, lay headquarters, in a grove of willows, protected on one side by a bluff, but exposed and vulnerable from the north, west, and south.

When they passed the upper end of the hay marsh, they were still at some distance from headquarters. Ren fanned his men on and stopped once more for a look to the rear. That

time he saw a pin point of light slightly to the left of the
bigger fire. It looked like Frank and Flint had succeeded in
backfiring. He went on with his party, which then followed the
horseshoe bend of the creek around the point. A moment
later they pulled down once more. Off in the sooty distance
lay the grove that sheltered headquarters, the tower of the
windmill rising above the trees. There was no evidence of
disturbance, no alien sound in the night.

"You figured it right, Joe," Ren told Garnet. "Fowler
sent a little bunch ahead to set that fire on Eden. This and
the Crank Creek hay's the only way they could hit us hard
enough to hurt. At least we got here first."

"Think it could be the sheep again?" Pete Farraday said
uneasily.

"Could be," Ren admitted, "but I doubt it. Chance could
keep goin' without them. If he lost this—" He did not
need to conclude the statement.

They rode in slowly, hallooing the house to reassure the
men there. Then they came in among the trees and rode
the last distance, a dozen men to add their support to the
half dozen already there.

Eden had arrived about a half hour earlier, and Chance
had already taken steps. Armed to the teeth, the cook,
roustabout, blacksmith, and a general hand, kept at headquarters because he had grown too old to work cattle, were
posted at lookout points, ready to sound a warning. Somehow Eden had got Chance moved to a hasty barricade on the
upstairs porch, which commanded the sweep of the creek
through the grove and the buildings on the stream's far side.

Ren joined them there for a moment, saying, "Glad to
have you with us, Varley, and I sure wish I didn't have bad
news. Your hay's burnin' right now. They set it afire to pull
us off down there while they hit here."

The men, both too old and one too crippled for this, lay
with their rifles poked through the apertures in the banister.

Ren heard Chance groan while Eden looked up at him, slack-featured.

"Well," Eden mused, "guess I'd rather learn it here than down there trustin' the mangy sons."

"You'll have company," Chance said grimly. "There's no way we can save our own hay, either."

Ren swung away, convinced of that himself. He liked what Chance had already done and only built onto it, posting men around the grove with instructions to fall back into cover when the fight began. Then he went out to the windmill that drew on the creek and climbed the tower to the tank platform. From there he could watch the outer distance in all directions in the strengthening light of the stars and of the half-moon that hung over the west.

But there were two blind spots, the creek growth upstream and down, into which his gaze could not penetrate. Unlike the grove, it was a narrow belt of trees and underbrush. A large force could travel in it unobserved if it moved in file.

His first alert was open and out on the flat, two dots that grew larger and became horses and riders precipitately moving his way. They would be Watson and Hollister, scurrying in from their attempt to minimize Fowler's fire. They waved their hats as they neared, afraid of being fired on by mistake. He did the same, hoping they would notice him. Apparently they did, for they settled and came thundering on to the grove.

They had to pass nearly under him, and he called to stop them. When they had halted directly below, he yelled, "What kind of luck?"

"We made it," Watson answered. "Draft from the big fire sucked our little one its way like a calf runnin' to its ma."

"Good. See anybody?"

"That's what growed wings on our heels," Farraday put in. "We climbed Rattlesnake Rock, afterwards. The light let us see our side clear down to the narrows, since the smoke all blowed the other way. Big bunch was crossin' toward the Kettles, down there."

"Ah," Ren said softly. "They'll cross the hills and try comin' in from above us. How many?"

"Must've been a couple of dozen."

"They can muster twice that, so there's another bunch around. Maybe more. Good work, boys. Take care of your horses and find a place to dig in."

The intelligence increased Ren's uneasiness. It went against his grain to wait passively to be hit while his imagination pictured the unlimited possibilities open to Fowler. He descended the ladder and found Landusky, who was off to his left, and told him to take up his watch from the tower. He found Fanning and Jewett and told them to move down the creek a couple of hundred years. They were to sound a warning if the enemy tried to slip in under cover, then fall back posthaste.

He started walking up the creek alone.

He went farther out than he had wanted to send the others and presently halted where a little glade broke the line of trees and brush. From his position he could also see the narrow floor of the valley to the edges of the hugging bluffs.

His eyes ached from staring across the obscurity when the punch of a gunshot cut through the stillness downstream. He hauled around, wondering if the observed party had skulked along the far edge of the hills instead of crossing them. The one shot seemed to have half a dozen echoes, which then swelled into a steady crashing of angry guns.

It drew him magnetically, until another thought slid into his mind and held him where he was. The party observed at the narrows did not know it had been seen. This attack was a feint by another bunch, designed to tie up Two C and open its rear to a surprise assault by the other group. He waited with the percussions beating his ears like hammers. If he dared to make the gamble, he might rip the entrails out of the second bunch. If he was right—while, if he was wrong—

He went scuttling under the trees toward the ranch compound. If he was guessing correctly, Fowler's stratagem had worked so far. Nearly all the men left on this side of the grove had gone across to join the skirmish line on the other. He found Fanning, who told him he and Jewett had barely reached their outpost down the creek when they heard the raiders moving upstream in the brush. They had fired warning shots and fallen back to the grove, as instructed, and now the enemy had spread out in the cover on the flat.

Ren tapped half a dozen men and took them with him up the creek, farther than he had gone previously. They carried rifles, which had guided him in choosing them, and he had picked one up for himself, with a reserve of ammunition. Anyone trying to attack from this direction would have to stick to the valley, for the sidehills above the cliffs were too rugged to be traversed easily. He had brought his men to a point he knew well, where an hourglass stricture narrowed the area and interrupted travel on the west side of the creek.

Concealed in the rocks at the base of the east bluff, he wondered if he was following a sound hunch or sheer lunacy. The crackling racket down the stream rendered their ears useless, but a dozen eyes keenly searched the area up the creek.

Landusky noticed them first and made a motion with his arm. Then Ren saw them emerge from the obscurity, the first riders coming on at a stealthy walk. He had won the gamble, and if his luck held he stood to break the back of the attack almost before it was launched.

The men had their orders and waited calmly, rifles lined on the enlarging party up there. Arched backs and upright heads showed that the oncomers' full attention was focused on the fighting at the compound. The angle relating them blunted as they moved more nearly abreast Ren's position, and something began to file Ren's nerves. Link Fowler led them, but he had begun to recognize others, men from Cat Track, Hat, War Bonnet. In spite of his own seering anger, he could not open up on the latter like Indians and cut them down.

When they were squarely off from the covering rifles, he sent his voice across the night.

"Freeze, you sons of shitepokes, or a lot of you are dead!"

He knew he had thrown it away, that out there were men not above exploiting any advantage. There was no order, but those who rode with a man between them and the menacing rifles sent their horses crashing into the creek cover. Those left exposed were forced to follow the best they could, and Ren's shot brought a roar of guns on both sides of him. He heard Fowler shouting, while bullets sprayed the brush and trees along the creek. In a moment a scathing gunfire came back from over there.

Ren felt his lips tighten on his teeth while he levered and fired. He had denied Fowler the advantage of surprise and could force him to fight his way to the compound, but he had to fall back in that direction himself. They were four to one against him. If they got below him, they could wipe him out.

He called quietly to Landusky, on his left. "Pass the word to start workin' in, Frank."

Landusky shot again before he answered. "Yeah. I'm glad you done it that way, though. My stomach turned on me, too, at the last minute."

Without loosening the pressure, the little Two C squad began to slip from rock to rock and behind brush clumps and trees, ever moving a little closer to the distant ranch buildings. Fowler's force seemed to have moved the horses back out of danger, and dismounted men kept up the same gradual movement down the creek. But none of them was bold enough to try getting ahead to prevent the withdrawal.

The fighting beyond the compound was still at peak intensity, and presently the two parts fused into one jarring uproar. Then Fowler saw the opportunity Ren had hoped he would miss. The far bluff had receded from the creek, permitting passage on that side. When a sudden slackening in the shooting warned Ren that they were crossing to get ahead, he snapped an order to break off and run for it.

Discerning his intention, the mustanger's men crossed the stream en masse, their objective the open side of the compound. It was neck and neck, and Ren hoped the abrupt halt in the shooting up here would warn the compound that it might be open in the rear. They were in the horseshoe bend of the creek, finally, and he and his men had the inside track, which helped. The big grove loomed ahead, and if there were pickets on this side now, they discerned the situation and did not shoot. Plunging into the compound, Ren yelled for help and splashed over the creek.

He was in time to see at least a dozen men racing toward him from upstream. His own had scattered on his flanks, and they cut loose. The volley sent the figures out there scampering, and in a moment they were down in the cover.

Ren lost no time strengthening the line on this side of the compound and joining it to the one on the west. That thinned the whole line, but resulted in his skirmishers ringing the headquarters grove in a wide U, with its ends anchored on the east bluff. The raiders were soon aware that it was the curved back of a porcupine.

With the fight stabilized, Ren withdrew and made his way to the ranch house across the creek. Climbing to the upstairs porch, where he had left Chance and Eden, he found it deserted. He knew why. The position had been taken when it seemed that half a dozen men would have to defend the place, and the attack had been brought to a halt at the edge of the grove. Chance had not been content to stay here out of the fighting, and somehow he had got himself to the firing line.

That canceled the need to tell him what had been taking place out of his sight. Ren went to the storeroom and there in the darkness broke out more ammunition. The supply was limited, and its exhaustion would deliver Two C automatically to its enemies. He could carry what was left easily, and with it he moved out to distribute it along the line.

He found Chance forted in the understructure of the windmill tower, at the edge of the grove. The position commanded the basin road and a sweep of ground on either side, and he was holding off four or five men out there. He turned his head when Ren crawled up to him.

"Pearce and I are exchanging compliments," he said.

"He out there?"

Chance shot again. "I think another's Roddy."

"Fowler brought another bunch down the creek."

"What're our chances?"

"I'd be lyin' if I called 'em good. We've won a standoff, so far, but it can't last. We've shot up half our shells."

"I know."

Ren completed his rounds, relieved to find that while there had been many close calls, Two C had so far suffered no casualties. It had compact, internal lines of communication and dense cover, while the raiders were flung out along a much longer line sparsely protected. As he moved from place to place, Ren warned against any unnecessary shooting.

This finished, he took position in the center of the line, so inured to the hard, sharp fragments of sound he seemed not to hear them. The spring dawn could not be more than a couple of hours away, and he wondered what effect that would have on the situation. It depended on how well Fowler and Jerome could keep up the fighting spirit of their recruits, he supposed. The latter were men blinded, but earnestly moved, by their feeling against the sheep, a passion not so easily sustained as Fowler's venality and the false pride prodding Jerome.

The first man hit chanced to be not far from Ren, who heard the quick, choked outcry. It came from his left, and when he crawled over he found Pete Farraday lying motionless in the rifle pit he had built himself. Even as Ren hovered there, another bullet thunked into the ground. On the heels of that came a third shot, and another man cried out. Ren swung his head in time to see a flash of fire at the brink of the bluff behind the house.

They had got a sharpshooter or so up there to shoot into the rear of the Two C line, aiming at the gun flashes. He yelled a warning and told the nearer men to pass it on. Hollister came crawling up, and Ren told him to look out for the men who had been hit. Rising, he made a bold, open run across the creek and on to the house. He wasn't fired on, which proved the sharpshooters were guiding their aim by the muzzle flash of the guns below them. Two could play that game.

He reached the second floor of the house and went on to the attic, where a dormer window opened on the bluff side. He knocked away the glass and looked out just in time to see the flash of a gun muzzle, across from him and not much higher. Shouldering the rifle, he flung a shot toward it. Another red streak winked for an instant, just beyond the first. Before he could jack another shell into the chamber of the rifle, a bullet drilled into the window casing against which his shoulder rested. He knew they had spotted him.

CHAPTER NINETEEN

He stood with his attention split between the two positions, over there, wondering if there were yet others. They seemed to be waiting on him, now, and for long moments he watched with straining eyes, his jaded ears almost muted to the distant gunfire. Then flame thinly slit the night, across from him, and he shot and shifted his position. He drew fire, shot again, then pulled deeper into the room while fire spots leaped back and forth, over there. He held his fire, thereafter, hoping he could fool them into thinking they had discouraged him or knocked him out of the fight.

Their shooting stopped, and he moved back to the window, hungrily waiting. And they waited, through another wearing interval, before one of them dared to try another shot into the yard. He was ready for it, and his gun echoed the other. The man seemed to have raised up to aim, for a vague, uncontrolled figure staggered into sight on the rim, then sank down. Even as this happened, the other man shot. Ren was ready and fired in the first split-second of the gun flash.

He didn't know if he had made a hit, but that was the last of the firing from that position. Yet he would have to stay here and keep it neutralized for the protection of his own men. It was wearing, when fury still spent itself in the grove, but he settled down to it.

His realization that dawn was near came with another awareness. For the past few minutes, the shooting in the grove had been diminishing in intensity. At first he feared it meant Two C was running out of ammunition, yet there was a more hopeful possibility. If the raiders decided to break off the attack, they would be apt to do it before daylight.

But would they do that without one final work of vengeance, the torching of the huge hay marsh they had so far neglected? He dared not take a chance.

Hurrying down through the house, he entered the yard and went on to the tower of the windmill. Chance seemed not to have changed position since he was last there, but he was all right and very much in the fight. Moving up to him, Ren said, "Think they're pulling out? There doesn't seem to be so much shooting."

"I've noticed, and I think that's the reason. There was some yelling out there, a while ago. Couldn't understand much of it, but I got the idea that everybody but Crown and Fowler's mustangers're ready to call it a draw for this time."

"If Jerome and Fowler reach the same conclusion, they're going to set fire to the hay before they pull stakes."

Chance muttered, "That's highly probable, but there's no helping it."

"Maybe there is."

"How?"

But Ren was gone.

He sensed that the moment of balance had come, a point when, with the right move, he might turn the tide. Losses and sagging morale were not the only reason some of the night raiders were pulling out of it. They had come a long distance from their base, and their ammunition supply was not unlimited. Ren went scurrying along the line, picking up every other man so as not to weaken any one point, and he kept it up until he had gathered five.

These he took with him to the north end of the line, where it anchored on the bluff. Throwing them in there, he moved that whole end outward, bending and bringing it into position between Jerome's sector and the hay lands down the creek.

It was a risky, desperate move, but it exposed Jerome to a flank attack. If it worked and drove him off, he would be inclined to move up the creek to join Fowler's contingent there. The easiest retreat for them, afterward, would be on up the valley, then over the Kettles the way Fowler had come in. By the time they could descend to the basin again, Ren knew, he could have men scattered along the edge of the marsh down there. That might discourage any further attempt at destruction.

He had swung the shifted line within range of Jerome's position before he let it open fire. The raining barrage, coming in from a new angle, brought yelps of surprise from the other side, which found itself confronted by an enemy twice as extended as before. Ren detected Jerome's heavy yell as he tried to checkmate the move. But Ren had advanced his own men as far as he dared, and in a moment they were drawing fire. The advent of good light would have to decide the rest.

He had taken the exposed end of the line, and it was some ten minutes later when something off to his right caught his attention. He turned his head to stare into the still obscured distance, but now could see nothing. He decided it had been his imagination, but it bothered him. If Jerome had decided to pull out, he might try to send a man slipping around the end to make sure the marsh was set on fire before he withdrew his fighting force. The chance was too great to dismiss, and Ren began to work his way to the rear.

Presently he dared to rise to a stand for a better look. Muscle tightened at the base of his skull. Farther off, a man was walking steadily toward the marsh.

It had been another good guess, and he dared not throw this one away. One match could still deal a crippling blow to Two C. He started after the fellow, moving quietly but swiftly, now and then losing sight of him when sagebrush or rock intervened. The man thought he had got away unnoticed and made no effort to hide himself as he hurried on. If warned, he would only lose himself and wait to do his damage. That left one chance. Ren slid swiftly over the sandy earth, trying to draw near enough for an effective shot.

His motive was more compelling than that of the man ahead, and the gap narrowed. He began to trot, and when it incited no change ahead, he picked his spot. In a moment the man would be at some distance from the nearest cover, permitting a second shot if the first failed of its mark. And then the moment came, and, stopping, he lifted the butt of the rifle to his shoulder.

It was as before. He could not cut down a man in cold blood. He shot, sending the bullet ripping across the distance to snap in the fellow's ears. It was the man's decision whether to bolt for it, or to turn and fight. He chose the latter, throwing himself around. A gun spat fire before he shot again. The man's arms shot upward. It was not a signal of surrender. He made a crazy, knee-folding dip of the body and then fell to the ground.

Ren went on warily, but it was no trick. The man was down on his back, staring up into the dawn-dusted sky. Ren let out an explosive breath.

"Roddy!"

A horrible, ripping groan came out of Roddy. But the fight was gone from him, the life was running out. The gun he had let go lay beyond reach. Ren dropped to his knees beside him. The front of Roddy's shirt, breast high, was dark and wet. His breathing gurgled.

"You," Roddy said on a gagging breath. "Might of known —it'd be you. God damn you."

"You'd do better prayin', Hunk. You're hit hard."

"I—know it. Ren—tell Rita—" Roddy coughed.

Urgently, Ren said, "Tell her what?"

With effort, Roddy said, "She—ain't a bad—girl. Tell her—
Red Bluff."

Sharply, Ren said, "Her youngster's there?"

"My—sister's—the name's Jordan—"

Blood came gushing out, then, and a moment later Hunk
Roddy was dead.

Ren rose to a stand, wondering what infinitesimal spot
of decency in Roddy Rita had reached. Then he went striding
back toward the fight, which was peaking in its fury. He
understood the change well before he could rejoin his men.
The light would be strengthening swiftly from now on. The
raiders were breaking off, hoping to pull out, and Two C
had surged on to the offensive.

By the time he reached the grove, Jerome's position had
been evacuated, and the fight was raging along the upper
creek. But when he came in among the trees, he grew
aware of a brisk exchange of shots, just ahead. At the windmill tower, he thought, breaking into a run. Seconds later he
realized that while the main attacking force had retreated
along the upper creek, a few of them had lingered, hidden
until the bulk of Two C had moved upstream in pursuit.

They had Chance besieged in the tower, intending to kill
him, and then go in and burn the buildings.

Ren swerved toward the tower, and a rifle crashed on his
left, with a bullet knocking the hat from his head. He went
sprawling headlong while more shots cut the air where he
had been.

Link Fowler's voice yelled, "Here's Ren Tyler!"

Ren lay pressed to the ground. It was typical of Fowler's
trickery to lie doggo until the chance opened to rush in for
the kill. Now he saw the possibility of getting Two C's owner
and ramrod in one action. He was urging whatever men he
had kept with him to make good on the opportunity.

Again hot lead raked the ground by him, and Ren wondered if he could live long enough to get behind the closest

tree. He bellied forward, expecting at any instant to feel the bite of a bullet. Then, in a moment, he had the heavy bole of an old cottonwood between him and Fowler. His lips tightened on his teeth.

Fowler's party had found cover at the edge of the talus under the east bluff, Ren discerned. If he could be patient long enough, he might lead them to think they had knocked him out. He lay with hot, searching eyes, hearing the percussive rattle of the fighting up the creek. It seemed a great while before a man raised up, over there. It was Fowler. When Ren didn't shoot, Fowler grew encouraged. He motioned, and then two others joined him in a rush toward the tower and Chance.

"Wrong way, Fowler!" Ren shouted, shoving up.

Fowler heeled toward him, shooting fast. Boldly exposed, knowing Chance couldn't survive another moment unless he made his shot good, Ren came around the tree. He shot simultaneously with Fowler. A bullet cut hotly through the side of his shirt. Fowler staggered back, fired again, and fell. Another man went down, telling Ren that Chance was still in the fight. The third man wheeled and went bolting up the creek. He had gone only a few strides when Chance dropped him. All three, Ren discovered, were dead.

Ren ran on to where Chance lay under the tower. The crippled man hadn't been hit, but he looked grateful. He said tightly, "I had some bad moments. I thought you'd all taken off after the main bunch."

"Roddy tried to burn the hay," Ren told him. "He didn't cut it. And you can't do any more good here. Let me help you to the house."

Chance nodded, and Ren assisted him across the compound. The fighting had stopped, except for scattered shots. Presently the men were returning to headquarters. One of the first was Abe Jewett, whose grim face held a look of satisfaction.

"Looks like they all run out on Fowler and Jerome. Maybe Jerome would have run too, but he couldn't. He's dead, out there on the flat."

Ren and Chance shared Abe's satisfaction. With the ring-leaders gone, the association would disintegrate. That would end the deadline, the black-listing, and eventually, Ren hoped, the prejudice against the sheep. What Rita could tell would help get Lands' herders out of the Alkali jail. But nobody considered it an occasion to celebrate. Pete Farraday was dead and Jim Fanning wounded in the thigh, both victims of Link Fowler and the others involved in the ambitious and vicious plot. The raiders apparently had got their wounded away, but there were three other dead men scattered around the grove. Two were mustangers, and one had ridden for Crown.

Ren started a man for Alkali, for they needed not only the doctor but the sheriff. He had the bodies moved into shelter and covered, and the scattered horses, some abandoned by riders now dead, were gathered and cared for. By then the cook had breakfast ready, and Two C was moving back to normal. Joe Garnet and Varley Eden ate with the crew, thus breaking bread with erstwhile enemies, and Chance called them into his office before they left for home.

There was a twinkle in his eyes when he said, "You lost your hay last night, Varley."

"Yeah," the old man agreed, "and I reckon I got off pretty easy, at that."

"You've squared accounts as far as I'm concerned, you and Joe both. But I'm warning you. I'm keeping my sheep. In fact, after haying, I'm bringing them down on the stubble. That'll be right next to you both."

"How do you reckon they'd do on my place?" Eden said.

Garnet looked at him and grinned. "Be damned if I ain't been havin' the same wonder."

"They're the answer to the times," Chance assured them.

"Just like cultivated hay was twenty years ago, when I came here."

Hesitantly, awkwardly, they offered their hands, which Chance took readily. Ren followed the two visitors out and stopped Garnet at the foot of the steps.

"Roddy told me where Rita's boy is," he said.

"Did he? She said he knew. At his sister's, somewhere."

"Red Bluff, and her name's Jordan. Tell her, will you?"

Garnet looked at the ground, then back at Ren. "I reckon you know what I said about you not bein' welcome don't stand no more."

"Hoped you'd say that."

"Then why not ride over with me and tell her, yourself?"

"Thanks. Hoped you'd say that, too."